The Ancient Anarchist

AND OTHER STORIES

BHAASITA ATHANI

ISBN 979-8-88909-301-5

Contents

Preface

Since this is the first book I have put together and decided to publish, I thought I should talk about myself a little bit first.

I was born and brought up in Bangalore, India. Books and literature were always talked about in my home, and there always was an artistic air around me in my family when I was growing up. I started reading novels early on, at the age of eight.

I started out with the usual children's books like Famous Five and Goosebumps, but slowly progressed into reading Sherlock Holmes when I was in my early teens. It wasn't until I had read Stephen King that I was really inspired to start writing my own stories.

I remember that my initial motivation to explore writing fiction was a need to understand perspectives that were radically different from mine. So, my first attempt at fiction was a story about Maximilian Robespierre, who was a post-revolution French dictator. We had a section on him in our history textbook when I was in the ninth grade. I remember reading about his obsessive use of the Guillotine and how he mercilessly beheaded anyone he perceived to be his enemy. I found it utterly horrifying that he thought beheading people was the most appropriate way to get rid of them. But, at the same time, I was also fascinated by him as an individual. I was puzzled by what it was that could have led him to become a monster. There was also an element of irony in his story that was interesting to me: he too was killed by the same machine he used to kill his enemies. So I fictionalized the incidents that I read about him and created a story about Robespierre's journey to the Guillotine.

It was through this experiment that I realized my passion for telling stories. As I grew into adulthood, I started reading the works of writers like Kafka and Chekhov. These two writers have had a major influence on me. As I wrote bigger stories and constructed more complex narratives, I began to fall in love with the art of putting words together to make meaning and create worlds.

– Bhaasita Athani

December 7, 2022

The Day Before

The convict sat – on his dirty bunk, inside his dark, little cell – staring at a lightning shaped crack in the wall. They had given him a cell with a relatively nice view to spend his last day. That was his last wish.

But he hadn't looked out of the window in a while. He sat staring at the crack with a blizzard of thoughts in his head. *Tomorrow, by this time, they will probably be doing my autopsy. Why is the crack lightning shaped? Most of the cracks I've seen are either like spider webs or lightning...fascinating. How much would a hanging possibly hurt? How did this crack get here? Did some idiot make a futile attempt at breaking out and give up? Or was he caught making this stupid move and sent to another cell?*

He just didn't feel like looking out of the window. As he sat there, lost in thought, he heard a metallic knock on his cell-door. Two men wearing black suits and black ties stood there with insincere smiles. They seemed to think they looked spiffy, having no idea how much dust there was on their suits. It looked horrendous due to the unfortunate lighting.

"Hello, professor! We were hoping we could have a small chit chat with you before…you know." said one of them. The other one gave a hesitant grin as if to say, "If you don't mind".

"Uh…okay" said the convict.

One of the men unlocked the door and came in while the other one picked up two folding chairs and came in behind him. The convict was surprised to see the lack of caution with which the men entered. He could just snatch one of the chairs and beat the two of them to death. He had nothing holding him back anyway. But, the two of them seemed sickeningly confident that something like that wouldn't happen. As they sat down at a comfortable distance away from the convict, he noticed that one of the ties was in fact a dark shade of blue and not black.

"So, professor, how're you holding up? You don't seem to like the window." said the one with the black tie. There was a polite pause and then, blue tie joined.

"We don't wanna take away any of your time, so if you would rather be left alone, please do tell us."

The convict wasn't sure if he was allowed to talk to his prosecutors. But they literally couldn't cause him any more harm so, *what the hell*, he thought. He knew and used both their names at least a zillion times over the last couple of years, but now, he simply could not remember them.

"It's alright." said the convict.

"Thanks. We really don't have any agenda we want to push. We just wanted to have a chance to have a personal conversation with you and see how you're feeling." said blue tie.

"Well…I'm just thinking about things I guess." said the convict.

"It must be exceptionally hard for you considering the fact that you're innocent." said black tie.

There was a cold and unpleasant silence for the next few seconds. The convict's face – that was absolutely expressionless up until then – came to life with a look of helpless confusion. Blue tie let out an irritated sigh, leaning forward uncomfortably.

"That…was not planned." said blue tie, looking down at the floor. Black tie, with a puzzled look, shifted in his seat, not knowing what to do next.

"Tell you what…it's almost lunch time. How about we all finish eating and then talk so that we don't have to be interrupted?" said blue tie. The two of them got up and left hurriedly, leaving their chairs where they were. The convict – with eyes showing a lack of words – could hear angry whispering as the two men walked away from his cell. *What on earth had just happened?*

All the expected questions charged into the convict's head. He desperately tried to push them out so that he could make space for a plan. *Is there a way I could continue on that crack? Maybe I could use the chairs! Or what if I use the chairs as weapons and ambush the two of them when they get back and open the door? No, no! I would only be further incriminating myself. I should use my power of language and reason to cut a deal with them. I am, afterall, a professor. What deal would they agree to that they didn't for two damn years?! No…I should move them with a powerful speech. Yes! I am in extraordinary circumstances. That ought to give my words some sort of special value.*

All this while, he hadn't noticed his lunch that had been pushed into his cell. He went over, picked it up and sat on one of the chairs. As he ate, he composed his speech and his arguments. *I would have to sound angry and wise at the same time. I should have an air of superiority. I should seem indifferent to the fact that I am going to die tomorrow.*

"Where is your sense of honor? How could you respect yourselves, being upholders of this ghastly system of injustice?! How can you live with yourselves after using an innocent, responsible man as a scapegoat?! Millions of people sleep at night because of the faith they have in this bloodthirsty system of yours. I wonder how you people sleep at night!" the convict muttered to himself as he ate his lunch.

He pushed the empty plate out of his cell and walked over to the window. There was another block being constructed. Although he couldn't see it, he could hear the sounds of construction. The laborers were yelling at each other in their normalized rude voices. There was a breeze and the yelling stopped…and then it continued.

Some time passed and the two men returned. The convict heard them open the door and enter. He didn't turn away from the window. He sensed them observing him for a few seconds before he heard them sit. Then, he turned around, walked to his bunk and sat comfortably.

"Professor, I hope you enjoyed your lunch. So, where were we?" said black tie.

"Oh, let's see…I think we stopped at you informing me of your knowledge of my innocence." said the convict with an undetectably nervous smile on his face.

"Right. Um…yeah." stammered black tie.

"Would you like to elaborate…on that?" asked the convict.

"How…in what way would you like us to elaborate, professor?" asked blue tie.

"You wanted to know how I feel, right? That's why you came here? I wanna know how you feel, about using an innocent, responsible citizen like me…as a scapegoat! I would've thought, you gentlemen have some honor and are better than tha-" the convict was interrupted by a disapproving chuckle from blue tie.

"Scapegoat? Forgive me, professor, but I think that's a bit of a harsh word." said blue tie.

"Harsh?! What the hell are you talking about?" cried the convict in disbelief.

"I'm afraid you're getting a little too emotional about this, professor. There's no need for that, don't you think?" said black tie.

"Emotional! I am going to die tomorrow for something that I didn't do. Try getting that through your thick skull!" yelled the convict. A guard peeped through the glass on the door. Blue tie waved him away.

"I understand what you are going through. I cannot even begin to imagine the kind of mental torment that you are experiencing. But, let's try to have a logical discussion about this. You're a rational person aren't you? I just don't think you are seeing this whole thing the right way." said blue tie.

"Oh please…enlighten me!" said the convict.

"Okay. So if I hear you correctly, you think we used you as a scapegoat in order to prove some bigger point about how strong the state is and flex its muscle. But, I'm afraid that's not the case. What we really did was, push you out of your box and make you do something profoundly honorable. Isn't that a good thing, professor?" said blue tie.

"I don't understand." said the convict. His head was spinning.

"You are just not looking at the big picture, sir." said black tie, adjusting his collar.

"What do you mean big picture? The whole point of having a justice system is to ensure justice to each and every individual. What other big picture could there be?" said the convict.

"In an ideal world, that would be true, sir. But we don't live in a perfect world. Wouldn't you agree that we have to extract the best outcomes out of whatever world we are provided with?" said blue tie.

"I suppose…" said the convict.

"Okay, so logically we are on the same page. You agree with our argument. You're just letting your instincts get in the way." said black tie, with the compassionate eyes of a parent.

The convict just listened in silence. He hadn't prepared for this. It wasn't supposed to go like this.

"So…let's…let's just say you're right. How am I doing something noble here by getting myself slaughtered?" asked the convict, helplessly.

"The crime you were convicted of is obviously a very serious one. It is quite rampant in our society and its consequences are too expensive to bear. Now, we know because of prior data, that there are a significant number of individuals who are potential perpetrators of this crime, and it is our moral duty to do everything in our hands to stop them. Wouldn't you agree? I'm sure you would. Now, it so happens that the burden of doing that is on the justice system, which is far from flawless. What does one do in this situation? We have a problem, an imperfect environment to solve it, and the best possible outcome to extract." said blue tie.

The convict leaned back and took a deep breath. He let out a sigh of deep disappointment. He was disappointed in himself…because somewhere – deep down – he was being convinced. He was letting go.

"The act of convicting you and giving you a death sentence is one solution. One of the best kinds. Let me tell you why. These potential perpetrators are now convinced that their actions will have serious consequences and that they will be punished for being anti-social elements. Reinforcement of that simple belief goes an unimaginably long way in preventing the crime. You see, it doesn't really matter if you actually did commit the crime or not, because in comparison with the unbelievable good that your self-sacrifice achieves, your personal loss is really negligible." said blue tie.

"This is what I meant when I said big picture, sir. Now, do you realize that you come across as a tad selfish when you talk about the injustice you are facing? We are all living for a higher purpose, professor. You of all people should know that. YOU are better than this. You are a martyr." said black tie.

The convict had no words. His mind was completely numb.

"With civilization, there comes an implicit consensus, professor. Compromise of the self for the greater good of society. You are nothing but a demonstration of this consensus. Your sacrifice will save countless lives. These lives will never know you. But their souls will secretly be proud of you, and thankful for you. Keep that in mind." said blue tie.

"You know one thing for sure," said black tie, as the two of them stood up to leave." We will always salute you for your actions and everyone who knows that you are innocent will remember you for the hero that you are." He tapped the convict on the shoulder as if to say goodbye and blue tie nodded respectfully. The two men locked the door behind them and left.

When the convict was young, he had once run all the way from his house to the bus stop to catch a bus. He had missed it. He felt bad about missing the bus, but glad that he didn't have to run any longer. That was exactly how he felt now. The relief of giving up.

He had decided earlier that he wouldn't sleep his last night alive, because he wanted to experience every second of his last few hours. So, he got up, sat on one of the chairs, and continued staring at the crack.

* * *

Arbhutha's Revelation

The merciless afternoon sun dominated the sky. Arbhutha lay in his den upside down staring at his paws. The black stripes that ran all over his arms and the rest of his orange body were always fascinating for him to look at. They looked just like the shadows cast by trees on the sand.

He loved to sit around at home and think about his stripes and the other colorful things he saw around him. But everytime he caught himself daydreaming for too long, he heard his mother's voice in his head accompanied by his brothers' cruel laughs.

"This is why you will never learn the ways of your kind! All you ever do is sit around staring at the trees and the rocks. You think you can survive in these jungles with this kind of an attitude? Get over your silliness for heaven's sake! All your brothers have grown up. It's time you do as well." His mother often yelled at him when he was a child. He was a slow learner when it came to hunting. He would always get lost in thought right when he had to take action. This habit of his drove his family right out of their minds.

As he grew older, his mother stopped yelling at him, but his older brother took her place. Everytime they caught a deer – which was considered a luxury in his family – Arbhutha's brother would make him wait till all the other brothers had finished eating their share. Then, when Arbhutha looked – in horror – at the insultingly small piece of meat leftover for him, his brother would come up to his ears and say, "Maybe hunger is the only thing that will drive you to learn our ways."

His mother sat at a distance and watched indifferently as Arbhutha was mistreated and humiliated this way by his own brothers throughout his childhood. One day, he decided that he did not belong to this family of bullies and sadists. He was destined to live alone and wander through the forests, adhering to his own lifestyle. Sure, he would sometimes go for days on end without food, but he was happy as long as he didn't have to conform to the ways of his family.

He rolled over and stood up, shaking off his drowsiness. He hadn't eaten in more than two days and the last thing he'd eaten was a slim old duck. He did not believe in the supremacy of eating deer. He thought it was an unnecessary waste of his time and energy. From what he recalled, he never even liked the way they tasted. The only food he liked were rabbits and ducks. They were reliable and just enough for him. These were his ways. So what if this made him thin? At least he had the originality and authenticity to create his own lifestyle.

He walked out of his den and sat down, looking around. His stomach gurgled. It was time for him to go hunting. Although Arbhutha was a foodie just like his ancestors, he didn't really enjoy the process of actually getting his food. He never quite understood why the prey that he hunted always struggled and screamed when he caught them. *Don't they know that whatever is happening is supposed to be happening? What part of this is a surprise to them?* This was something that never ceased to amuse and agitate him.

Rabbits had always been his favorite when it came to taste. They had just the right consistency and texture. But they gave him a hard time. He hardly ever caught one, but was overjoyed when he did. Ducks, on the other hand, were kind of his staple diet. He very rarely failed to catch one. But, he wasn't the biggest fan when it came to how they tasted. Their annoying feathers were always stuck in his teeth and he'd often spend hours trying to get them out.

He started walking towards the thickets in front of his den. He would always first look around for rabbits and only after he was confident of his bad luck would he proceed to the stream. He groaned and snapped as a leaf tickled his ear.

It became cold and dark as soon as he stepped into the thickets. This built a kind of chilling suspense for him everytime he went hunting. He avoided all the sticks and twigs in his way as he looked around cautiously. No matter how careful he was, the bushes and leaves rubbing against his body would often give him away to his prey. He sometimes even had to crawl on the ground so that the leaves didn't reach him. Sometimes, the leaves would turn brittle and fall to the ground in big lumps. This would happen for days and Arbhutha found it extremely difficult to find his food on these occasions. Luckily, today was not one of those days.

The faint sunlight shivered on the ground as a light breeze hit the trees. The shadows looked just like Arbhutha's stripes. He wondered if he looked like a piece of the ground crawling amidst the bushes. Just as he was about to get lost in that thought, he saw something move, out of the corner of his eye. He slowly looked around, and voila! It was a fat little rabbit munching on something near a big tree. The tree behind it gave Arbhutha good contrast and he could make out exactly how many days he could survive on this meal. He turned just a little, got even lower with his jaw almost brushing against the ground and started moving towards the rabbit. As he took his first step, the forest became deafeningly quiet. The Rabbit stopped eating and stiffened up. Arbhutha let out a growl and jumped. The rabbit had just enough time to look at him and jump out of the way. Arbhutha rammed into the tree behind where the rabbit was, yelped and fell on his front.

He stood up and looked around frantically. Everything was blurred from the impact. But he could see that the rabbit had escaped. He clenched his teeth out of anger. *Oh what a damn embarrassment! Could it get any worse than this? You have truly hit rock bottom!* His brother's voice played in his head. He could see his mother's disappointed look.

He looked at the tree, hungry and livid. He didn't know what to do. *I guess ducks are all that I'm good for,* he thought.

Just as he was about to turn towards the stream, an unusual smell hit him. He was a little confused. Normally, he could not smell his prey until he first saw them from a distance. This kind of an overt smell was very new to him. He sniffed and started walking towards the smell. After a rather long stretch of bushes, the forest suddenly opened up to a large lake. *How had he never come here before?* He wondered. As he looked around, his eyes caught something that he thought was too good to be true. A large, white animal was drinking water out of the lake. He had heard about these animals in stories that his mother used to tell him and his brothers. When his mother was a child, her family lived near a human settlement. These humans were timid and helpless when they were alone, but scary and monstrous when they came in groups. They were just like wild dogs. Although his mother's family knew that they were dangerous, they chose to live near them, because these humans brought big, slow animals called cows near the forest. These cows would sometimes be far apart from each other and if his mother managed to catch one of them, the entire family could eat and have full stomachs for a long, long time.

What Arbhutha was seeing was one of these creatures. A cow. His stomach gurgled ferociously. He felt a strong sense of pride fill his entire body. He had never felt this way before. Strong, capable and menacing. He felt like one of his kind.

Arbhutha could not control himself any longer. He let out a piercing roar and ran towards the cow. As he ran, he saw the cow look at him and then something very strange happened. The cow did not run away. It did not even try. It just stood there, first with a look of fear in its eyes. But this look then changed into something that Arbhutha had not seen in any animal before. It was a look of submission.

Arbhutha stopped just short of the cow, making sure that he was blocking its way. He could not contain his excitement. He looked at the cow and laughed louder than he ever had. He realized as he was laughing that he sounded just like his brothers. He could not believe that this was happening. The cow kneeled and put its head down.

"I am going to rip you apart and drink your blood!" announced Arbhutha. He had no idea why he was saying this out loud. It just felt right. The cow looked up, right into Arbhutha's eyes.

"Alright…but please hear me out before you do that. I understand that you are hungry and frustrated. You must not have had anything to eat in a long time. But, you see, I have a little boy waiting for me at home. He must be really hungry by now too, expecting me to go back and feed him. He's a mama's boy, poor kid." said the cow, as she let out a weak chuckle, with tears filling up her eyes." This might sound really unreasonable to you, but I'll ask you anyway. Will you allow me to go back and feed him, stay with him this one night, teach him how to live without his mother, and come back? You will have to stay hungry for just a day and then your stomach will be full for longer than you can imagine…"

Arbhutha was astounded. In all his years, he had not encountered or experienced anything remotely like this. He did not know what to say.

"Wh…what are you, out of your mind? Are you trying to insult me? How stupid would that be, to let a fine meal just walk away? It's unthinkable!" growled Arbhutha.

"Of course, you would feel that way. But, you have to believe me. I could never be dishonest. For better or worse, it just is not in me. Just consider what I am saying for a minute. You had a mother too and she would have definitely sacrificed her life trying to feed you when you were a child. Please…just try and put yourself in my son's place." said the cow, with a look of helpless desperation in her eyes.

Something about what she said struck a chord with Arbhutha. He started feeling things he had never felt in his life. Nothing had prepared him for the situation that he was in.

"If you do not come here tomorrow, right after sunrise, I will come searching for you and kill your entire family!" said Arbhutha shaking with anger. Just as the cow was about to say something, he turned and ran away.

* * *

As Arbhutha walked back to his den, with his stomach still gurgling, all the pride and strength that he had felt just a while ago had vanished. He instead felt a toxic and powerful feeling of shame gripping him from head to toe. His mother and brothers had been right all along. But, he also felt alone and deprived. He felt envious. He was envious of that cow's child. It had a mother that so deeply cared about its well-being. The cow did not care if her child was tough, or if it learnt "the ways of its kind". Her love for her child was simple. Arbhutha had never had that kind of love in his life. All his family cared about was whether he was like them or not. They constantly made him conscious of his weaknesses.

But, he thought, *maybe they were right all along. Maybe I am destined to be weak and impotent.* When he decided to leave his family, his mother had said to him, "Our ancestors always said that there are two kinds within us. Ones that win and ones that lose. We have watched the losers among us starve and die right in front of our eyes. Nobody grieves for them. Me and your brothers tried very hard to turn you into a winner. We tried our best."

Arbhutha walked into the darkness of his den and lied down. A loser, that's what he was. He couldn't bear the gurgling in his stomach. He shut his eyes. The cow was not going to come back. He would die a slow and painful death, he thought as he fell asleep.

When Arbhutha woke up, it was the next morning. He felt too weak to leave his den. He just sat there, looking out into the bristling bushes. There was a sound he began to hear from in between the bushes. *It is probably another predator,* he thought, indifferently.

As he sat there, recollecting his past and the life he'd lived, the sound from the bushes got closer and closer. Arbhutha paid absolutely no attention to it until a figure appeared out of the bushes. He could not believe his eyes. It was the cow. There she stood, with the same, genuine look in her eyes. But, the fear had vanished from her demeanor. She was content…almost even happy.

The cow walked up to Arbhutha, inside his den.

"I came to the lake first thing in the morning… you weren't there. I thought maybe something had happened to you and came looking. But, I'm glad to see that you're well. I apologize for having kept you waiting for this long. You must really be starving by now. Anyway…here I am, flesh and blood. I'm all yours." she said and sat down…waiting to be killed and eaten. There wasn't an ounce of contempt in her eyes.

Arbhutha was devastated. His childhood flashed in front of his eyes. Every meal he had ever had was right in front of him. Thousands of petrified, lifeless eyes, frozen in their painful screams for help. Thousands of mangled limbs that once stumbled and struggled to stand in their infancy. He saw himself and his brothers tear through these eyes and pull apart these limbs, one after another, competing for a bigger piece. All of a sudden, his body, that was light from starvation, began to feel too heavy for his feet. He felt like he would break through the rocks underneath him and fall into the ground. Finally, a tear rolled down his face and dripped down from the tip of one of his whiskers.

"How could I possibly kill you?…" said Arbhutha, looking into the cow's confused eyes." You and I are siblings…children of this forest. How could I harm you, and live with myself?"

Arbhutha walked past the cow and didn't look back. He kept walking. His mind was clear. He felt elevated. As he walked through the forest, the trees finally opened up to a cliff. Arbhutha walked up to the edge, looked down and took a deep breath.

Post-script: This story is inspired by the famous Kannada narrative-poem 'Govina Haadu' composed by an anonymous poet, some time in the 18th or 19th century. While the original poem is written from the cow's perspective, this story is a reimagination of the events in the poem from the tiger's perspective, without altering the events themselves.

✳ ✳ ✳

The Rescue Dog

Jimmy was a stray dog who lived on the mean streets of Bangalore. He was brown in color with black spots all over. He was a dog who thoroughly enjoyed his life. He would roam around all day, looking at the wondrous things these humans were doing, be it driving around in cars, bikes or getting on buses. His most favorite pastime was sitting in front of shops or bakeries and looking at all the food, being prepared and kept on display.

He slept on a skywalk, which in his opinion was the biggest luxury a stray dog could have. Sometimes, a security guard would shoo him away from there, so on those days, he would sleep in front of a temple nearby. Each day, as he woke up, many people would be walking on the skywalk and one of these people – a man wearing a tie – would give Jimmy a whole packet of Marie Gold biscuits. This was Jimmy's breakfast.

He would finish eating the biscuits and come down the skywalk, where many college students would pet him and take pictures of him. This always made him feel very special. Then, he would start his routine of roaming around, sitting in front of shops and picking fights with other stray dogs.

Everyday, in the morning, he would see pedigree dogs walking with their owners. They were all very beautiful too. Some of them had rich, golden hair, some of them looked big and strong with ears that were always erect, and some of them – Jimmy's favorite – had no tails! The ones with no tails always made Jimmy laugh. These pedigree dogs always winced at the sight of Jimmy and other stray dogs. They seemed to especially hate Jimmy because unlike other stray dogs, he wasn't jealous of these pedigrees, he didn't look at them as his superiors.

One day, as Jimmy walked with Raja – another stray dog whom he had fought and later befriended recently – he came across one of these pedigrees. This one was the type that had golden hair. Once they had passed him, Raja sighed.

"We are really unlucky, don't you think?" said Raja.

"What? Why do you think so?" replied Jimmy, turning towards Raja.

"Look at those pedigrees! They live such royal lives, while we just run around being chased away by people." replied Raja.

Jimmy didn't say anything.

"I hope we get rescued. That's our only hope of ever being like them." said Raja.

"What does that mean?" asked Jimmy.

"Look, when someone who wants a dog picks one of us up from the street instead of buying a pedigree, it's called rescuing."

"Oh, you mean someone would just pick us up, take us to their home and keep us like they keep those pedigrees?!"

"Yeah…well, that's not how it usually works. A guy comes around in a big truck sometimes and whatever stray dogs are in that area get picked up. They are the lucky ones. They get taught special tricks and get trained by this man so that they can impress the people who want to take these dogs home."

"Lucky ones? Wouldn't you want to just be free and roam around instead of being taught funny tricks so that people can lock you up in their homes?" asked Jimmy, rather confused.

"What a silly simpleton you are! You need to be of value in this world! Instead of learning new things and serving as a companion to dog's best friends, you want to roam around, being smelly and lead an absolutely meaningless life? What can I tell you? There is such a thing as purpose in life, you need to become aware of that." barked Raja and walked away, frowning.

This conversation had turned Jimmy's world upside down in a minute. Had he wasted his life so far just wandering around and looking at bakeries? Was he supposed to be of use to these humans? So, were these pedigrees actually superior to him?

He had trouble sleeping that night. The next day, he woke up and sat waiting for the man with the biscuits. The man came as usual and after he laid down the biscuits for Jimmy, Jimmy started feeling uneasy about eating it. He got these biscuits without earning them. Does this mean nobody expected anything of him? Was he a worthless dog? After a while of thinking, he ate up the biscuits and went down the skywalk. He saw the girls that usually took pictures of him, taking pictures of a pedigree puppy. This made his heart skip a beat with a kind of pain he had never felt in his life – jealousy. It truly felt horrible.

Later, as he sat in front of a bakery staring at the food, he didn't feel the immense excitement and joy that he felt every day. He felt like a burden to the humans standing around him. One man threw a biscuit at Jimmy and it landed on the floor. Jimmy felt so offended at this that he walked away without eating it. He had never done something like that before.

Just as he was walking back towards the skywalk, Raja came running towards Jimmy.

"Jimmy! Come, follow me. You will not regret this."

Raja's tone sounded serious, so Jimmy followed him without a word. As they ran, Jimmy saw a big truck into which half a dozen stray dogs were being put. Jimmy stopped at this sight for a second.

"What? Why did you stop? Jimmy, this isn't the time for your silly games. Just shut up and come. You may never get this opportunity again!" growled Raja.

Jimmy hesitantly followed Raja. As they got closer to the truck, a man wearing a cap saw them. He came to them with two small biscuits and two leashes. The dogs were then put into separate cages inside the truck.

As the truck was moving, Jimmy looked around nervously. Raja was in the cage next to his. He looked very excited and happy. Every other dog in the truck looked happy to Jimmy.

"Relax, Jimmy. Everything will be fine." said Raja.

Jimmy put his head down and closed his eyes. He was awakened by the sound of the truck door opening. All the dogs were soon taken out, put into separate rooms with grilled walls inside a big building. Every room had multiple bowls in them for food and water.

After some time, a woman came into Jimmy's room, put him on a leash and took him outside. Here, he was given a bath. This was definitely not a pleasant experience for Jimmy. Cold water was blasted at him from a pipe, and a strong, unpleasant-smelling substance was rubbed all over his body and cleansed off again with cold water.

After his bath, he was put back in his room. All his natural scent had vanished. Now, he was smelling like a mango tree. He hated this new smell of himself – it made him uncomfortable. The woman came back with a bag, poured something into one of his bowls and left. Jimmy went and sniffed at what had been poured. It had no smell at all! He tasted it and it was tasteless and even hard to eat as it was so small in size. He ate half the bowl and sat in a corner, waiting to see what would happen next.

After a while, he saw Raja being taken out to the middle of the big building so that all the dogs could see him. He went closer to his gate to see what was happening.

The man who had taken Raja out stood in front of Raja, pointed at him and yelled out a sharp, short sound. Nothing happened. He yelled again, still nothing. Raja just stood staring at the man with his head tilted. The man yelled a third time and this time he pushed Raja's buttocks down so that Raja was now in a sitting position. Now, the man gave him a treat. Raja wagged his tail.

Jimmy turned away, went to a corner and lied down. This was definitely not a good idea.

* * *

The Ancient Anarchist

Chapter 1

About 11,000 years ago, in the forests, there was a tribe called Pamboo. They were hunter - gatherers. They were quite a large tribe in terms of their population. They had a population that fluctuated around 200. They stayed in one location for about a month before they moved.

The Pamboo tribe had four elders and they were the leaders of the tribe. Their authority couldn't be questioned. After every hunt, all the meat was to be submitted to the elders and they would divide and distribute the meat depending upon the needs of each family.

Dundur was one member of this tribe. He was a middle – aged man and he had no family. His weakness at hunting had caused this loneliness of his. No girl's parents were willing to give their daughter to him as he wouldn't be able to take care of a family. But, he did have some very good friends that didn't ostracize him for not being able to hunt well and always encouraged him to try.

One day, as all the men were getting ready to go hunt for the day, Dundur sat in his hut, nervous as ever. His friend, Bukpa came in.

"Come on, Dundur, we're leaving." said Bukpa.

"Yes." said Dundur quickly and got up.

The two came out and joined their other friend, Mabdub. The three of them were always together while hunting. Bukpa and Mabdub gave Dundur some simple tasks to make him feel important.

The men entered the thick forests and spread out. Mabdub had spotted a deer drinking water from a nearby stream yesterday, so the three were going there today. The three of them went in that direction and walked for about a mile. They heard the soft sound of water and Mabdub nodded his head indicating that this was the one. They hid behind a bush and sat, waiting. About an hour had passed and suddenly a small deer approached the stream. It was a calf. Mabdub and Bukpa saw this and whispered among themselves, looking at Dundur. Dundur looked at them anxiously. After their brief discussion, Bukpa looked at Dundur.

"You're taking this kill." said Bukpa.

"Quickly, there's no time. It's only a matter of seconds before the mother comes." said Mabdub before Dundur could protest.

Dundur sighed and drew out an arrow from the sling he had on his back. He positioned it on the bow and took aim. He looked at the calf. He couldn't see it as a kill. He saw it as a little baby that had come to the stream for a drink of water and after that, would go back to his mother, stick with his herd, grow up into an adult and live a good life. Now, he was going to get killed and would be served as food for a fat kid in the tribe. He took his shot and closed his eyes, hoping that he had missed. He heard a painful yelp and the sound of a tender body falling into the water. His friends were rejoicing. He opened his eyes and the tears that were collecting inside, ran down his face. He wiped his face immediately.

They took the calf and went back to the settlement. The other men had deer, rabbits, birds and other such animals. The three of them stood in line for submission and waited.

"We're so proud of you, Dundur." said Bukpa.

"Yes, you were amazing today." agreed Mabdub.

"Mmhm." replied Dundur.

"What? Aren't you happy?" asked Mabdub.

"Not really. It was still a calf. It had a life to live, you know? We just stole it away from its mother. She's probably looking for it now." said Dundur.

"For all we know, one of these men might have hit the mother while she was looking. Look, we can't think about these things. We have a life to live too, right?" said Bukpa.

"I don't even eat the meat. I just eat the fruits and berries that women gather. How am I gonna live with myself after killing a young calf for no reason at all?" replied Dundur, frustrated.

"So what if you don't eat it? Someone else in the tribe will. We have to take care of each other, not just ourselves. That's why we have a tribe. And where are you going with this, anyway? Are you suggesting that you don't want to hunt anymore or something? You just want to sit around in your hut all day and be called a free rider? You'll be ostracized by everyone. That's why we are trying so hard to make you good at hunting, don't you see?" said Mabdub, wanting to end this discussion.

"Whatever. I don't know what to do anymore." said Dundur and walked away from the line.

Soon, it was night and everybody gathered outside the huts for dinner. Food was kept on flattened tree barks that were laid down. There was all kinds of meat and in the end, there were fruits, berries and some leaves. Dundur went straight to that end and served himself.

There were dances around a bonfire every night. But, Dundur didn't watch them or participate in them. He went back to his hut with his food. Mabdub and Bukpa saw him and joined him in his hut.

"You know, those Gaongoos get as much meat as they want. There is no regulation for them. They don't even hunt, they just make some weapons. We are forced to use them and we work hard to hunt and in the end, we have to deal with this kind of limitation on food." said Bukpa angrily. Mabdub waved his fist in agreement.

"Why doesn't anybody point this out to the elders? Everybody is always complaining about it." asked Dundur.

"The elders know. They are in bed with the Gaongoo family because their weapons are needed in case there is a war." said Mabdub, leaning forward so that nobody can overhear.

"But still, they can't use that as an excuse for giving them more food than others. How much of this injustice can you take?" asked Dundur.

"Nobody wants to question the elders, Dundur." said Mabdub.

"They will if they're not alone, right? What if we convince everybody to have a meeting about this with the elders? Then the elders would have to agree because it would be them and the Gaongoos against the entire tribe." said Dundur. There was a brief moment of silence.

"We could try." said Bukpa.

"What if we ask some people today and they could spread the word?" asked Mabdub.

"We'll go to every hut tonight before everybody sleeps and tell them that there will be a meeting about this tomorrow and that everybody will participate in it. That would make them want to come." said Dundur.

The three of them agreed on this plan and prepared to campaign.

* * *

Chapter 2

The tribe always kept the bonfire burning at night. They did this to protect themselves from nocturnal animals. All the activities of the night were over and everybody was inside their hut. Nobody had gone to sleep yet as that would happen after a small whistle by a whistleman assigned by the elders.

Dundur, Bukpa and Mabdub came outside. They had a script prepared for their little campaign.

"Let's spread out. You tell your next door neighbors and I'll tell mine. We'll keep doing it till we find someone who might spread the word." said Dundur.

The other two said all right and branched out. Dundur went to his neighbor's hut and asked for permission to enter.

"Oh, Dundur! Come in, come in. What brings you here at this time? Do you need something?" asked his neighbor.

"Oh no, comrade. I am here for a much bigger reason." said Dundur, his eyes sparkling.

"Really? And what is that?" asked his neighbor. His wife, who usually avoided Dundur, and his kids came to listen. They were curious. It seemed like Dundur had something interesting to say.

"Let me ask you something, how was dinner tonight?" asked Dundur, with slight sarcasm in his tone of voice.

"It was really good, I enjoyed it. I wish I could have had more." replied the neighbor.

"Oh I see, so why didn't you then? Why didn't you have more?" asked Dundur. The neighbor and his family looked at each other, laughing.

"What do you mean? You know why, because the limits laid down by the elders don't allow it." said the neighbor, confused about whatever was going on.

"Oh, then you should also know that the Gaongoo family has no limits. They can eat as much meat as they want even if there is a shortage and the rest of us have to eat less. What do you think of that?" asked Dundur.

"Well…I do resent it, to be honest with you. But, they have such allowances because they make weapons for hunting and in case there is a war…" said the neighbor. But in his tone, Dundur could sense that he didn't believe that theory at heart and was only living with it because he had no other choice. Dundur smiled.

"Do you seriously believe that, my friend? Let's just imagine that their family didn't exist. Would we just run out of weapons? No, of course not. We would make our own weapons as we actually are right now. I know you have your own hand-made weapons. You don't have to hide it, I do too." said Dundur. The neighbor shifted a little with discomfort at hearing this.

"Yes, I do," muttered the neighbor.

"Of course you do. Nobody could trust that wretched family's weapons because all of them are badly made and we are forced to use them. So, they get to make bad weapons, have the elders impose those weapons on us and get unlimited meat. Whereas, the rest of us have to use those weapons at our own risk and have limits on our food. Does this seem like a fair deal to you?" asked Dundur, breathless due to the passion with which he had said all this.

The neighbor was speechless. He did know that he had been facing injustice, but he hadn't thought about it in depth and certainly hadn't heard the problem so well articulated.

"What do we do?" asked the neighbor, quietly.

"Tomorrow, let's have a meeting with the elders. Spread the word to as many people as you can. We'll point this out to them and they'll have to listen because it's them against the entire tribe." said Dundur.

"Yes, Dundur. As you say." said the neighbor.

Not many people really slept that night. People were moving from hut to hut on tiptoes informing each other about the meeting. The whistleman came out and saw this. But, he didn't know what to do. So, he just did what he was supposed to do and blew the whistle. Nobody had noticed him up until then. Everybody froze. Dundur saw Bukpa walk up to the whistleman, and tell him something. His body language told Dundur what he was talking about. The whistleman nodded and went back to his hut.

They were safe. The elders had heard the whistle and had gone to sleep. Everybody was careful not to disturb any hut that belonged to the Gaongoo family.

After they had got the message out to everyone, they sent them back to their huts and the three came back to Dundur's hut.

"So, what's the plan for tomorrow?" asked Mabdub.

"You should be the one that talks first at the meeting, Dundur. This whole thing was your initiative." said Bukpa.

"I know, I will speak first, but I can't be the only one that speaks. I'll open and then after we hear what the elders and the family have to say, you and everybody else have to speak up too." said Dundur.

"Of course."

They wished each other luck for tomorrow and went to bed. There were only a couple more hours left before dawn.

Chapter 3

The next day, even before Dundur was awake, the entire tribe had assembled in front of the four elders' huts. Dundur walked over to the front of the crowd where Bukpa and Mabdub were already standing. He noticed that the Gaongoo family was standing separately, a little distance away from the crowd.

"What's that about?" asked Dundur.

"Apparently, one of them noticed all the hustle and bustle outside last night. They might have taken a guess." replied Bukpa.

The whistleman looked at the sky and gave out the morning whistle from within the crowd. All four elders came out almost simultaneously. There was muffled conversation in the crowd.

Even though there were four elders, in reality, only one of them took all the decisions. The other three advised him if they thought his judgment was faulty, which they usually didn't.

"So, what is all this about?" asked the chief elder, in his hoarse voice.

Dundur cleared his throat and stepped forward.

"My lord, I am Dundur and we have all gathered here today to express a problem we have all been facing for a long time. We don't agree with the mandatory use of weapons made only by the Gaongoo family as they are poor in quality and we prefer to use our own weapons. But, that's not the main reason we are here. We are more concerned about the limits we have to accept on our food and meat everyday and we also resent the fact that the Gaongoo family faces no such limits. I think this luxury that they are enjoying at our cost is unjustified due to the reason I just mentioned." said Dundur, all in one breath.

There was silence all around him. The only sounds he could hear were from the morning birds and trees shaking due to the wind with their leaves rubbing against each other. Everyone in the crowd was silent. Such an incident had never really happened in their lives. No one had organized a meeting to express disagreement with the elders.

"But, this is a custom we have followed for generations, Dundur. The Gaongoo family has always been the one to supply weapons to the tribe. They may be slightly poor in quality as they make large amounts of these weapons and it's hard not to make mistakes. We can't just do away with such a tradition." said the chief elder.

The head member of the Gaongoo family stepped forward.

"My lord, I don't know if you paid attention to everything this man said right now, but he implied that he has his own weapons and so does almost everybody else in the tribe. This is against the rules laid down by you, the honorable elders and your ancestors. We have been trying to tell you this for a long time." he said.

"We all know that, but it's only for our own safety that we are suggesting a change in that rule. We understand that it's hard for you to make that many weapons perfectly. It would just be easier and more efficient for everyone to make their own weapons. This would ensure perfection as everyone would have to make only one or few perfect weapons, you see? We are not doing this out of contempt for you." said Dundur.

"Oh, what would you know about weapons, you fool?! You can't even eat meat, let alone hunt. You cry at the sight of killed animals." yelled the head Gaongoo.

At this point, Dundur's friends and the rest of the crowd joined in.

"It doesn't take a hunter to see the injustice we are facing. So what if Dundur doesn't hunt well? We do, and we agree with him." yelled Mabdub.

"Yes, yes! We agree with Dundur." shouted the crowd, raising their hands in approval.

One of the other elders went to the chief and said something in his ear. The chief raised his stick and everybody became silent.

"We understand that this is an issue that has to be resolved. We will find a solution and get back to you before today's hunt." said the chief.

"Yes, my lord." replied Dundur. Everybody took a bow.

The crowd dispersed and in some time, breakfast was distributed. Dundur sent one of his newly emerged followers to check the Gaongoo huts and if they were still receiving excess supplies. The man returned and said that the entire family had gone to the chief elder's hut to have breakfast with them. This seemed a little fishy to him, but he chose not to think about it until he had heard the decision taken by the elders.

After breakfast, everyone got prepared for that day's hunt and assembled outside again. The elder's came out and the chief raised his stick.

"After a long discussion with my fellow elders, I have come to a conclusion. We shall allow the members of the tribe to use their own hand-made weapons only for the purpose of hunting. The Gaongoo family shall continue to make weapons and store them for war times. They shall no longer have the unlimited food supply that they used to, but will have a larger supply of meat than any other family. And, in case of war, you shall all be required to submit your weapons to us and we shall distribute it along with the Gaongoos' weapons as we will have to use everything we have. That's the end of this discussion. Disperse!" he said and raised his stick.

Dundur was not completely satisfied with this solution, but he decided not to protest against it as it was indeed a step in the right direction. He was going to keep quiet at least for now.

He passed on this instruction to everyone as they left for the hunt.

"What do you think is the next step? This certainly isn't the end. There is no way we are going to submit our weapons during war. That defeats the purpose." said Bukpa, as they walked into the forests.

"They are still getting a larger supply only because they make weapons for war times. If we submit our weapons too, how does that justify them still getting a larger supply. It just doesn't make any sense." said Mabdub.

"Those Gaongoos have always had a stranglehold over the elders. They must have manipulated them during their breakfast." said Bukpa.

"Look, it isn't true that the elders are very kind hearted, but are working under the pressure of the Gaongoos. The both of them need to work together to hold their power. They are interdependent." said Dundur.

"If you think about it, how does it make any sense that the chief elder's son grows up to be the next elder? How do we know that he is qualified for that job? That's why the elders are getting worse by the generations." said Mabdub.

"So many things are wrong about this tribe. Dundur is making me realize all these truths. We need to do something about all this." said Bukpa.

"We shall go one step at a time, my friends, one step at a time." said Dundur.

✳ ✳ ✳

Chapter 4

It wasn't even the next full moon before a new problem had arisen. The Gaongoos had started using poison to kill animals. They used a special herb that was poisonous at the end of their arrows so that the animal would die even if the arrow was slightly weak. This herb was available only to the Gaongoos as the elders had made an announcement that this herb should not be used by anyone else. If this herb was found in anyone's possession, they would be denied access to meat and would have to survive on fruits and berries until the elders said otherwise.

This enraged Dundur and his friends. Soon, the anger spread throughout the tribe.

"Just when we thought things were getting a little better...Something has to be done about this, shall we organize another meeting?" asked Bukpa, walking around restlessly in Dundur's hut.

"Yes, we should, but I don't think it is a good idea for me to take the lead on this one." replied Dundur, stroking his long beard.

"Why not?" asked Mabdub.

"I don't eat meat. I survive on fruits and berries anyway, so if I bring this up in front of the Gaongoos, they will point that out. It will dilute the issue." said Dundur.

"Who else is there? I mean you are right that it will be easy for them to manipulate the situation if a non-meat eater brings up this issue, but I don't see who else can take the lead on this one." said Mabdub.

"Why don't you two take this up? You're good hunters, the tribe knows that the two of you played an important role during our last meeting. Also, two people are better than one. The tribe will follow you and the Gaongoos won't be able to manipulate the elders' judgment." said Dundur.

Mabdub and Bukpa looked at Dundur in silence.

"But, there won't be as much unity in the tribe if you don't take the lead. They see something in you. You're not an ordinary guy, right? They see you as an eccentric. Although they won't admit it, the tribe likes eccentric people." said Bukpa.

"I will participate, but I will be in the background. I will take the lead in campaigning at night, but you guys will have to speak at the meeting." said Dundur.

Soon, it was night, and everyone was in their hut. The three of them got ready with their lines and left the hut. It was made very clear in their lines that this too was Dundur's idea. They spread out as usual and told each and every hut about another meeting. This time, they didn't let anybody else come out. The whole thing was done by the three of them. All the noise caused by everyone coming out the last time had woken up the Gaongoos and they didn't want that to happen again. If they got the chance to prepare, it would cause problems during the meeting.

Dundur went to his next door neighbor first.

"So, my friend, I'm sure you know why I'm here…" said Dundur.

"I do have a rough idea." said the neighbor.

"Oh, it is exactly what you think it is. It is about the poisonous herbs that the Gaongoos have been using." said Dundur.

"It's about time! We were waiting for you to bring it up. They are taking away all our prey with those herbs. The elders should either give us access to those herbs or take away their's." said the neighbor. It was evident that the whole tribe was waiting for Dundur to bring up this problem.

"Yes, yes, I agree. We shall hold a meeting tomorrow. But, this time, I shall not be speaking." said Dundur.

"Oh! Why is that? The whole tribe has placed trust in you." said the neighbor.

"I know that, but the problem is, if I talk about us not being able to hunt effectively, the Gaongoos will point out that I don't eat meat and that I am a bad hunter. You see how that will be problematic, don't you?" said Dundur.

"Yes, yes, I hadn't thought of that. Who will speak, then?" asked the neighbor.

"My two very good friends, Bukpa and Mabdub will be taking the lead. They are fantastic hunters and are respected members of the tribe. The elders will listen to them." said Dundur.

"Ah, that makes sense. We all know that they are your main men."

"I request you to treat them with as much love and respect as you did for me. Be just as unified and encouraging." said Dundur.

"Of course, Dundur."

It took them almost the whole night to finish telling everybody. By the time they were done, the sky was slightly blue indicating the arrival of the sun. They went to their huts to get some sleep.

Dundur lay on the floor of his hut and stared at the roof. Just a few days ago, he was just an annoying non meat-eater that everybody winced at. He thought everybody was fine with the elders and the Gaongoos running things the way they wanted to, at the cost of the tribe. As it turned out, he wasn't alone in his resentment of this injustice. All the people wanted was a voice leading them. It didn't even matter who that voice was to them, as long as he was going to express their concerns to the elders.

But, why hadn't something like this ever happened in the tribe? And why did the people so desperately want a leader? Why couldn't they express their concerns individually to the elders? What were they so afraid of?

Dundur sighed and closed his eyes. He slept until sunrise without any disturbance.

* * *

Chapter 5

When Dundur woke up, Bukpa was standing outside his hut. He looked anxious. Dundur came outside and the two started walking towards a small, still-forming crowd in front of the elders' huts.

"Are you ready?" asked Dundur.

"I think so. I don't know how you did it. It was hard enough standing next to you while you were speaking, and now we have to speak like that. This is the first time in the history of our tribe that something so new is happening. How come you don't feel threatened?" said Bukpa.

"Who says I don't? It is quite frightening, but then I don't have as much to lose as you do, so it was easier for me to take such a risk." said Dundur.

As they approached the crowd, they could see Mabdub talking to many people in the front. He didn't seem as frightened as Bukpa. He had also been the one to support Dundur when the Gaongoos had attacked Dundur during the previous meeting. He saw the two coming and went over to them.

"Listen, there has been a problem. They saw us again last night when we were campaigning." said Mabdub.

"What?! That's not possible. We made absolutely no sound." said Bukpa.

"Well, they did. But, that's not the worst part. They waited till we went back to our huts and then went and met with the elders. So, the elders know about today's meeting and its purpose." said Mabdub. Bukpa and Dundur looked at each other in dismay.

"But, they don't know that we know. The whistleman saw them going to the chief's hut and he told me this morning." said Mabdub.

"It's all right, just go according to the plan. If anything goes wrong, we'll handle it." said Dundur.

"What are we going to do if they have already thought of what to say to us? It isn't like last time, where it came as a shock to the elders." said Bukpa.

"I'll think of something." said Dundur.

By now, the entire tribe was out in front of the chief's hut. The three went and stood in their places. Mabdub was in front, Bukpa was next to him and Dundur was behind them.

The Gaongoos were standing separately just like the last time, but they all had smug smiles on their faces. Everybody sensed that there was going to be some serious trouble this time. The whistle was blown and out came the elders. They weren't shocked at all this time. The chief looked at Mabdub and raised his hand, indicating to him that he could start. So, it was worse than they thought. Mabdub stepped forward.

"My lord, I'm afraid we have another problem. We have all noticed that the Gaongoo family has gained access to a special poisonous herb that is capable of easily killing animals. This means that they can catch and kill more prey than anyone else in the tribe. They are effectively stealing our prey and we are all very upset by this. Since no one else has access to these herbs, we think what is going on is unfair." said Mabdub.

"Therefore, on behalf of the tribe, we propose that either everyone else should be granted access to these herbs, or the Gaongoos should lose their access. We prefer the former. That's all we have to say." said Bukpa.

The chief looked at the Gaongoo head.

"Oh, we have nothing to say, my lord. We trust in your judgment." said the head and smiled.

The chief looked back at the crowd.

"We have thought about this and we have already come to a conclusion regarding it. In fact, we had made up our minds about it even before you brought it up today. So, you don't have to wait to hear our decision. The Gaongoo family has always been the trusted one in the area of defense and weapons. We have granted them access to these herbs because they can be trusted with it as we know that they won't use it against their own tribe and also because they will have practice with it in case an enemy tribe attacks. Your previous request was considered legitimate by us because it was a safety concern. However, this is not. So, this proposal of your's is being rejected." said the chief, turned away and went back into his hut with the other three elders.

The crowd was awestruck. They did not know how to react to what had just happened. Things certainly hadn't gone as expected.

The head Gaongoo turned to the crowd.

"You heard him, didn't you, go on, disperse. What did you think? Just because they agreed to one of your pathetic 'requests', they will become your slaves and obey your commands? And you think they don't know that this too was a conspiracy hatched by that non-meat eating coward, Dundur? You are wrong if you do. They aren't fools like you. That's why they are the elders." he yelled.

At that point, Dundur made an astonishing move. He ran up to the raised stone platform that was meant for the elders and stood on it, facing everybody. Gasps could be heard from the crowd.

"My friends, are you going to listen to these people who have – from the very beginning – been favored by the elders at the cost of you, or are you going to listen to yourselves? Are you going to let this go just because the elders refused to support us?" said Dundur.

"No! No! No!" yelled the crowd. The same crowd that had gasped in horror at the sight of Dundur standing on the elders' platform, was now shouting in approval of what he was saying. The Gaongoos escaped back into their huts, frightened by what had just happened.

"These elders have always favored that family over the rest of us. Why should we listen to them, if they can't listen to us?" yelled Dundur.

"Yes! Yes! Yes!"

"We have almost two hundred people in this tribe. Are you telling me that nobody knows where these herbs are? Who knows where they are? Raise your hands!" said Dundur. Almost a quarter of the crowd raised their hands. Dundur laughed.

"Yes! Go ahead, all of you. Get as much of those herbs as you want and distribute them among yourselves. Don't leave any for the Gaongoos, they have had enough." said Dundur.

Immediately, the crowd ran together, screaming with new found freedom. Dundur, Bukpa and Mabdub went with them. Dundur was still processing what he had just done. There was no turning back now. They were going to get rid of the elders.

* * *

Chapter 6

That night, the three were back in Dundur's hut. They were drunk with adrenaline. Dundur sat on the floor, stroking his beard, smiling with pride.

"We cannot turn back now. We have to overthrow the elders." said Dundur.

"Yes. But, who would be the next elders?" asked Bukpa.

"You know the answer to that, of course. The entire tribe now trusts in one person and we are looking at him," said Mabdub, pointing at Dundur, "Dundur would be the next elder and the two of us would be his assistants."

"The three of us will be the next elders for sure, but that won't be permanent." said Dundur, getting up.

"What do you mean?" asked the other two, in unison.

"We shouldn't make the same mistakes as our ancestors. If we become the elders forever, what's to say that we won't become just like them – insensitive and selfish? So, what I'm suggesting is that we become elders temporarily, to ensure that the Gangoos don't take over, and then slowly take away their power and give it to everyone else in the tribe so that everybody has equal power in the tribe and no one can rule over others. Then, we quit as elders. So, we will have a tribe where everyone is free to do what they want to do, but still has the safety provided by the tribe. Do you understand what I'm saying?" said Dundur.

"That's very interesting." said Mabdub, after a brief moment of silence.

"Wow, I had never thought about it that way!" said Bukpa.

"But, this must be done very slowly. We cannot hurry. Over the next few days, the elders will inevitably do things that will upset the tribe. We will wait for at least three of such acts by them and then, we will say enough is enough and mobilize the tribe against the elders." said Dundur.

Tyab Gaongoo – the head of the Gaongoo family – waited in his hut, looking out of his doorway at Dundur's hut. He was waiting for his two friends to leave Dundur's hut. Soon, Bukpa and Mabdub came out of the hut, waved at Dundur and walked back to their respective huts. Tyab waited for some more time and then put on his top made of special long leaves. It was a gift given by the chief elder. He was going to meet the elders. He had had enough of Dundur's nonsense and had made a plan to end it. He walked over to the chief elder's hut and entered. He didn't need permission to enter.

"Ah! Tyab, what a surprise, we weren't expecting you at all." exclaimed the chief.

"Oh, I had a very urgent thing to talk about with you. It couldn't wait, really, so I just came over." said Tyab.

"What is it? Come, sit down." said the chief, looking puzzled. It was a phony gesture, of course. He had been thinking about the same thing.

"So, what do you think of this Dundur situation, chief?" asked Tyab, casually.

"Oh, I'm glad you brought it up, my friend. I must say I'm quite worried about the future of this tribe." said the chief, shaking his head dramatically. The chief's wife set down a plate full of fruits for the two of them.

"Have you thought about what to do about it?" asked Tyab.

"Oh, I have thought about……certain things, if you know what I mean." replied the chief, picking up a fruit.

"We can't get rid of him like……that, if that's what you are thinking. The tribe adores him and if they find out about us doing anything to him, it will be the end of us," said Tyab.

"Then what do you think we should do?"

"I have thought about it all day and I have made an elaborate plan. Listen carefully." said Tyab, leaning forward.

"I'm listening." said the chief, unconsciously imitating Tyab by leaning forward.

"This plan involves a big sacrifice. We are going to have to sacrifice our long alliance with the Jandunga tribe. I know this sounds insane, but when you listen to the whole plan, you will understand. As you know, Dundur's mother belonged to that tribe. What we are going to do is, we will tell the tribe that the Jandunga tribe has betrayed us and is going to wage war on us. We will have to attack them before they attack us. We will say that this is war and we cannot indulge in petty conflicts within the tribe. Also, it won't be long before some of our loyalists start connecting the fact about Dundur's mother with this and that connection will spread coldly throughout the tribe. The tribe will be forced to put their trust in us and that will be made easier by hearing the fact about Dundur's mother as that will dilute their adoration for him. If we don't do this just to keep an alliance, we will destroy the tribe from inside out.

If we sacrifice a dysfunctional alliance for this, we will not only regain the tribe's trust, but we will also effectively get rid of Dundur. What do you think of this?" said Tyab.

The chief leaned back and sighed as he hadn't even let his breath out when he was listening to Tyab. He chewed on the fruit he was holding in his hand as he thought about what he had just heard.

By the time he finished the fruit, Tyab had become impatient.

"Go on! What do you think?" he repeated.

The chief smiled.

"Tyab, my friend......what would I do without you?"

* * *

Chapter 7

The next day, Dundur woke up as usual to the whistle. As he was just getting up, the whistleman started making an announcement. He walked around so that he passed by every hut as he did it.

"Come one, come all! The elders are addressing the tribe now! Come out and assemble in front of the chief's hut. Come one, come all!" yelled the whistleman.

Well, that was quick, wasn't it thought Dundur to himself. He came out and saw everyone walking towards the chief's hut, murmuring among themselves. They saw him and bowed their heads. He bowed back. He found his two friends in the crowd and went over to them.

"So, what do you think this is?" asked Dundur.

"Strike one out of three, let's hope." replied Bukpa.

"That's what I thought when I heard the announcement." said Dundur.

"Oh, let's just hope it isn't anything too bad." said Mabdub.

They didn't stand in front of the crowd this time, they didn't want to look too ambitious. They stood somewhere in the middle and saw that the rest of the tribe clearly hadn't expected that. A few minutes later, there was another whistle and out came the elders. The chief had a smug smile on his face as he came out. However, it soon vanished voluntarily. Something seemed fishy about this whole thing to Dundur. The chief raised his stick and the crowd went silent.

"So…first I want to acknowledge that what happened yesterday was deeply resented by me and my fellow elders. But, that is not what we are here to talk about. We have a much bigger problem at hand. It is of great disappointment that our allied tribe, the Jandungas have betrayed us. They want to wage war against us."

Oh no! Thought Dundur. *This was bad, a cheap trick that was going to cost a lot.* The chief continued:

"We received this information from some of our loyalists while the rest of you were busy fighting against your own tribe! It is a matter of shame! Do you people know what would happen if they conquered us? They are barbaric! They won't allow you to hold meetings. We have a soft, accepting culture and some of you have taken advantage of it." he looked at Dundur as he said that." But, let's leave what has happened in the past and focus on the future. We have decided that we will attack them before they come for us. They won't see us coming. Now, you have an opportunity to prove your worth and your loyalty to this tribe. Forget about these petty conflicts within the tribe. This is war! And thanks to the Gaongoos – those you have all ganged up on – we are prepared. We can win, and we will win! Long live the Pamboo tribe!" said the chief and raised his stick.

Everybody was shouting with admiration for the chief. A man in the front shouted: "Long live," and everyone else shouted "the Pamboo tribe!" . Dundur,

Bukpa and Mabdub were pushed around as everyone cheered for the elders. Dundur turned around and ran to his hut. The other two ran after him.

"What the hell just happened there? That was unbelievable!" said Mabdub.

"This is wrong! This is so wrong! They've got the tribe back in their pockets." said Dundur.

"Do you think it's true? About the Jandungas?" asked Mabdub.

"Of course not! What would be the odds of that timing? I'm just shocked that they are willing to go that far." replied Dundur

"What are we gonna do now?" asked Mabdub.

"I don't know yet. But we can't be idle. We have to go around and tell everyone about this." said Dundur.

"Don't you think we should wait? They are still excited about that speech. We might seem desperate." said Mabdub.

"We'll wait till tonight. Anymore than that, we'll be too late." said Dundur.

After Mabdub and Bukpa left, Dundur sat, thinking about what to do. He was both worried and appalled by how the crowd had reacted to the speech. They knew that for generations, the Jandungas have always been loyal to their alliance with the Pamboos. Even the most stupid man will be able to work out what a cunning person the chief is. The Jandungas suddenly decide to attack the Pamboos when something unprecedented is happening?

He looked outside and saw everyone lining up to sign up as soldiers. He winced at the sight. As he looked outside, another frightening thought came to his mind.

Why hadn't Bukpa said anything after the speech? He was just standing behind Mabdub looking guilty while Dundur and Mabdub were talking. Dundur started feeling anxious.

He shaked away those thoughts and realized that even if the whole tribe gave up on him, his friends would always be beside him. He stayed in his hut the whole day as hunting was suspended for the next three days. They would all be eating fruits and berries collected by women as the men got ready for the battle.

Soon, it was dusk and Dundur ate his dinner, went back to his hut and waited for his friends. They were taking longer than usual. He started getting all sorts of bad thoughts about them. He started wondering if they were going to abandon him.

But, they came and he was relieved. They came inside. Both of them had gloomy expressions on their faces.

"What is it?" asked Dundur.

"Bukpa wants to tell you something." said Mabdub.

* * *

Chapter 8

"What is it?" asked Dundur, feeling a little uneasy.

"Look, Dundur, I don't want you to take this the wrong way, we have been friends for a long time and we shouldn't let this affect our friendship…"

"Just say what you want to say, Bukpa!" interrupted Dundur.

"I can't continue this struggle or campaign or whatever it is, with you and Mabdub." said Bukpa. There was absolute silence. Not even the sound of crickets could be heard around them. The kind of silence that makes you shift with discomfort.

"Why?" asked Dundur with latent anger in his voice.

"My wife has always been nagging me about what we were doing and now that we know about this war, I have come to agree with her." said Bukpa, briefly.

"You fool! It is not true! The elders are trying to manipulate us. You are falling prey for their nonsense?" growled Dundur, unable to hide his disappointment.

"What if it's true? What if we continue to not cooperate with the elders and the Jandungas attack us? I certainly will not be able to live with that." said Bukpa.

Dundur finally couldn't take this anymore. He stepped forward and pushed Bukpa with both hands. Mabdub jumped in to stop him.

"Go then! I knew you weren't committed to what we were doing anyway! Go away!" growled Dundur through his teeth.

Bukpa raised his hands as if to say, he was going to back off. He turned back and rushed back to his hut. Dundur stood there breathing heavily, waiting for his anger to go away. Before Mabdub could say anything, he said:

"Let's just forget that he was ever with us. We can't waste time now, you cover that side of the settlement, I'll cover this one." Mabdub went without a word.

Dundur went to his neighbor's hut.

"Dundur? What are you doing here at this time of the night?" asked his neighbor.

"I'm here to talk about what happened today at the meeting." replied Dundur.

"Hmm…what about it?" asked the neighbor.

"Of course you know what about it…the whole thing was made up to manipulate the tribe."

"Dundur! Enough is enough! We can no longer indulge in these silly fantasies of your's." said the neighbor. Dundur was shocked.

"What do you mean?"

"This is war, for god's sake! We can't do this anymore. How can you be so ignorant? The existence of our tribe is at stake and all you can think of is this? This is a time for all of us to be united against our enemy. We should support the elders in their decisions. Not go against them. You are making our tribe weak. Do you have any idea what goes on in the Jandunga tribe? You should, shouldn't you?"

"What? How should I know?" said Dundur, perplexed.

"Don't play dumb with me, Dundur. Everybody knows that your mother is from that tribe. We shouldn't be surprised about you trying to distract all of us. I needn't say anymore. Go away now! Don't try anything now, unless you want anything bad to happen to you!" said the neighbor and shooed him away.

Dundur was speechless. He couldn't understand how one speech by the chief could change the beliefs of this man so drastically. The neighbor, who could relate to Dundur and his problems, literally a few days ago, now treated him as an outsider. Why had this happened?

He saw Mabdub coming over to him with a worried look on his face.

"What happened?" asked Dundur, even though he somewhat knew.

"I just don't understand what's happened to everybody. I went to four huts, and they all talked to me as if I'm some sort of a criminal. They refused to even listen to what I had to say." said Mabdub, uncomprehendingly.

"That's what happened to me. Let's try more huts. We'll go together, and see if that's what everybody feels suddenly." said Dundur.

"I don't think that's a good idea, Dundur." said Mabdub.

"Why not?"

"Everybody seems to think you are some kind of an agent from the Jandungas. I think it's because your mother was from that tribe."

"But her marriage to my father was a symbol of the tribal alliance. It was decided by the elders." said Dundur, frustrated.

"Nobody is going to think about that now, Dundur. Those Gaongoos are smart. We need to stop for tonight." said Mabdub, decisively.

Dundur went to his hut without saying anything. That night, a million thoughts ran through Dundur's head. But, he wasn't angry or perplexed or shocked anymore. In fact, he didn't feel anything that night. He only thought.

He understood why the Gaongoos had a stranglehold on the tribe. They didn't just control everyone's thoughts, but also their feelings. This was what gave them their power. Their control over weapons and the elders' ability to control the war narrative gave them their invincible power.

As Dundur went to sleep that night, he knew that the next day, he was going to receive another piece of bad news.

* * *

Chapter 9

The next day, Dundur woke up before the morning whistle. He came outside his hut and sat down, leaning against the outer walls of his hut. He looked at the sunrise, as the dark blue sky turned red at first and then bright blue again. People were coming out of their huts, strangely excited about the war. Today was the day of the attack. Most of the men had signed up as the attacking soldiers. The families of these soldiers were embracing them with smiling faces. Some of these faces would certainly not be smiling later.

He had come to know that Bukpa had also signed up as a soldier. He was one of the men practicing the drills. He saw Mabdub come out of his hut. Mabdub saw Dundur, sighed nervously and started walking towards him.

As he approached him, Dundur looked him in the eye with no emotion at all. This scared Mabdub a little, but it looked as if he had practiced all night whatever he was going to say now.

"Good morning, Dundur." he said.

"Good morning."

"I have something to tell you…you are not going to be happy, but it is inevitable."

Dundur didn't say anything. Mabdub continued.

"I am signing up as an attacking soldier. I think us continuing on our mission of dethroning the elders and challenging the Gaongoos is no longer appropriate. I thought about what the people said to me last night and I think they are right. We should now be united as a tribe, against our enemy. Whatever might be the circumstances of this war, we can't afford to go against our tribe. I know you will not join me and I respect that. I hope you can respect my decision too." said Mabdub.

Dundur nodded slowly and looked away. Mabdub stood there for sometime and then turned away and started walking. Dundur looked back at him and saw him approach the commander of the practise drills. They had a small talk and then Mabdub joined the practice.

Dundur didn't even get up to eat breakfast. He just sat there, looking at the people with a combination of wonder and pity. They were all so thrilled and proud that their tribe had the upper hand in this war. Somehow, they gave no thought to the soldiers who were going to be putting their lives at stake even though they were their own family.

Finally, all the soldiers stood in positions, with their bows and arrows…They were standing in many rows with three people per row. Mabdub and Bukpa were standing next to each other. They saw Dundur and nodded. He nodded back.

The commander stood in his position, in front of everyone and yelled: "Long live!"

The rest of the soldiers yelled: "The Pamboo tribe!"

They started marching forward into the forests. The entire tribe started clapping. Dundur got up and went into his hut. The only thing he could think of was seeing his friends again.

The current settlement of the Jandunga tribe was half a day away from that of the Pamboo tribe. It was almost evening now, so they were almost there. The soldiers were now facing the fear that had somehow escaped them up until now.

Bukpa had a layer of sweat on his face that he hadn't wiped for a long time. He didn't want to get distracted. There was a vague pain in his chest. The moment he paid attention to it, it increased. It was fear. He didn't think it would be this frightening. He had imagined it very differently. He thought he would go there with immense bravery in his heart and they would all attack the elders' huts of the Jandunga tribe and return with immense pride back to their own tribe. But, bravery was anything but what he felt in his heart and he couldn't see pride anywhere in the distance. All he could see was doom. Chaos, pain and death.

He looked at Mabdub, who was on his right. All his feelings were reflected on Mabdub's face. Mabdub looked back at him and gave him a pitifully artificial smile.

"Don't worry, brother. We are going to do it." he said, his voice shaking.

"Yes." whispered Bukpa.

The commander raised his bow and everybody stopped. Bukpa could now hear the sounds of people talking and the bonfire already burning. They had reached! Bukpa's heart was beating out of his chest. *No! I cannot be afraid! I am a proud Pamboo and I shall do anything to serve my tribe!* He thought to himself in order to boost his morale.

For one moment, his surroundings fell silent altogether. There was not even the sound of leaves bristling against each other from the wind. The people were not talking anymore, and were bizarrely silent.

"ATTACK!" yelled the commander. And they ran forward with their arrows positioned with the bows.

They came out of the covering they were hiding behind to see the Jandungas' settlement. Everybody had vanished! All the people that seemed to be talking just a minute ago were nowhere to be seen. Bukpa's heart skipped a beat.

Whatever happened next proved that the Pamboo tribe had committed a terrible mistake by sending their troops. But the soldiers had no time to process the huge mistake they had made.

Armed soldiers of the Jandunga tribe appeared from behind every hut in the settlement and started shooting arrows. They largely outnumbered the Pamboos and had much stronger arrows.

Bukpa saw an arrow come flying at Mabdub and go right through his neck. Mabdub couldn't even scream out. He fell to the ground and was dead immediately with his mouth and eyes wide open.

Bukpa tried to go towards him but before he could put one step forward, an arrow struck him in the side. He felt his limbs go numb. It was a poisoned arrow. He collapsed to the ground and saw the Pamboo commander fall with an arrow in his eye. There were screams all around him. His eyes were going blurry when he saw a handful of Pamboo soldiers disappear back into the forest. Then, he finally blacked out and was dead.

* * *

Chapter 10

It was the next morning and Dundur was picking berries from a nearby tree with the women. He had decided that he wasn't going to go hunting anymore. He would instead help the women pluck fruits and berries and live a minimally participant life in the tribe. He was waiting for Mabdub and Bukpa to share his decision. He desperately wanted to talk to them. More importantly, he wanted to apologize to Bukpa. He shouldn't have acted the way he did with Bukpa.

The tribe was waiting eagerly for the arrival of their soldiers. Anxiety was slowly showing up on the faces of women. The men who didn't go were comforting women.

"What are you afraid of? Don't you know the strength of our soldiers? They will be back any moment now, don't worry."

Dundur tried to ignore the anxiety he himself was starting to experience. He had seen his friends hunt by his side, they were skilled. *They might be injured, but surely nothing worse could have happened*, he thought to himself.

That was when they came, the surviving soldiers. There were only six of them. They came running from inside the forest and collapsed in front of the bonfire. They were all breathing heavily. Dundur ran over to them and looked for Bukpa and Mabdub. They weren't there!

Before he could ask them anything, family members had gathered around them, pushing him aside. There were painful cries of grief from the crowd. There were cries of shock and horror.

One of the men pushed through the crowd and went to the chief's hut.

"Chief!" he yelled out.

The chief elder came out hurriedly, followed by the other elders.

"Oh! My dear man, what happened? Where are the rest of the soldiers?" asked the chief.

"Dead! All of them are dead! We are the only ones that survived. When we were running back, a voice yelled at us, 'Try this again and we will destroy your tribe, this is your first and last warning!' So, we don't have to worry about an attack from their side, my lord."

Dundur resisted the impulse to drop his basket of berries. His friends were dead. His only companions had left him. All the noise around him dimmed out in his ears. He could vaguely hear the chief say:

"Don't worry, my dear people, all is not lost. These tragedies do happen in times of war. We miscalculated. We must only build a bigger and better army and have a better strategy……"

He went into his hut and put all the berries he had collected into a deer-skin cloth. He took his bow and arrow (which he hadn't submitted) and a pot. These were all his belongings. He took them outside his hut and kept them there.

He then picked up a long dry leaf and went over to the bonfire. He lit the leaf on fire. Then, he came back over and set his hut on fire! The entire tribe looked in awe as his hut burnt in flames.

He took all his belongings and started walking. He disappeared into the forest and was never seen by the tribe again. He was going to live alone. He had had enough of this tribal life. He would use his bow and arrow for protection and would eat fruits and berries to survive. He walked on and on in search of caves. He had seen some nearby the tribe's previous settlement and as he knew that the tribe would never come back there, he would live in one of those caves alone, in peace.

He saw no point in living in that tribe. The only reason he had to be with them was so that he could be with his friends. But they were gone for good. He had lost them to war. A meaningless war. A war – in a way – caused by him. Maybe, if he hadn't started his struggle against the Gaongoos and the elders, all of this wouldn't have happened.

If he had just put his head down like the rest of the tribe in submission to his elders, maybe, his friends would still be with him. Could he live like that? It was too late now.

Now, he had no excuse to even try. So, he would live alone, on his own terms. Accountable to no one but himself.

It would be dangerous, it would be risky. But, it would be worth it. It would certainly be better than living in a herd.

As he thought about all this, he walked on away from his tribe, with a deer-skin bag on one shoulder, his bow and arrows on the other shoulder and a pot under his arms.

The people looked at the direction in which he had gone, perplexed and spellbound. They had just lost so many men to soldiers belonging to a tribe they thought they were in an alliance with until yesterday and now, one of them had set his hut on fire and had left the tribe. None of this had ever happened before. The chief didn't know what to say.

"What a coward!" yelled Tyab Gaongoo, breaking the silence.

"He causes all this unrest in the tribe with his silly meetings, and now that he knows we are at war, he leaves. He is a coward and he wasted all of our time."

"Yes, and I wouldn't be surprised if he told the Jandungas about our attack. Bloody spy! After all, his mother was a Jandunga." said another man.

"Yes, we should be glad he left."

The attention of the tribe soon came back to the wounded soldiers. They were taken to their huts to be treated and the chief continued with his speech.

Everybody got back to work.

✳ ✳ ✳

Bheema's Battle

Bheema was a soldier on the Kauravas' side in the Kurukshetra battle. His parents had named him after the brave and strong Bheema – the son of Kunthi, once they had decided that he would be a soldier after he grew up. Ironically, he was fighting against the army of the Pandavas in the battle.

Bheema had just returned from another war when he was summoned to fight this one. He was at home opening gifts – he had gathered from the conquered village – for his children, when his friend Pushkara came home and gave him the news. His wife had become very angry.

"Let's just run away from this kingdom and settle down in a forest somewhere," his wife, Vijayamathi had said.

However, he had managed to console her and convince her that he would return home safely after the war.

Bheema now stood on the battlefield with his closest comrades, waiting for instructions from the commander.

He just didn't understand the point of this war. The Kauravas and the Pandavas were cousins. Family members were going to be killing each other in this war. *They have the luck of being born in such powerful families and instead of using that as an advantage, they choose to tear their families apart.* He winced and sighed at this thought.

Suddenly, there was some commotion among his fellow soldiers. He asked Pushkara, who was standing next to him, what happened.

"Krishna and Arjuna have arrived," replied Pushkara in a dramatic tone.

Bheema raised his head and shielded his eyes from the sunlight to see and saw a chariot arrive on the enemy's side. Krishna, the lord himself was the charioteer. Bheema joined his palms, giving respect to Krishna.

"Why didn't we get Krishna? Isn't it a little unfair for him to side with the Pandavas? I worship him, literally," said Bheema to Pushkara.

"Well, we have Duryodhana, Karna, Dronacharya and Bheeshma, right?" replied Pushkara, uncomfortably.

"Oh yes, I suppose," said Bheema, not quite satisfied by the answer. But then, to speak against his masters would be a crime.

"So, how's the family?" asked Bheema after a brief moment of silence.

"Oh, they're okay. The wife nearly killed me for agreeing to come to this war. I mean, what else can I do? I can't refuse to fight it."

"Same with mine. They just don't understand."

"Would you two be quiet?! We are about to fight the biggest war in the history of humanity and you two are groveling about your wives" growled Ajaya, who was standing next to Pushkara.

The two paid little attention to this. Bheema took out a cloth and opened it up.

"Want some nuts?" he asked Pushkara.

"Sure" replied Pushkara and took about half the nuts in the cloth.

"Can you believe that in the next eighteen days, we'll most likely be dead?" said Pushkara, as he chewed.

"Hmm…crazy isn't it?" replied Bheema.

"When you think back, what are your fondest memories in life?" asked Pushkara.

"The day my second son was born, for sure. Wasn't there for the first one. What about your's?" replied Bheema.

"The day my father gifted me this sword" said Pushkara and held up his sword as it shone in the evening sunlight." It was my seventeenth birthday and my father gave this to me. 'Protect it as if your life depended on it.' he said."

Bheema looked at the setting sun, realizing that this might be the last time he ever witnesses a sunset. All of a sudden, he heard the sound of someone beginning to weep bitterly. He turned to see that Ajaya, the disciplined soldier, was on his knees, crying. He tried to intervene but Pushkara stopped him, shaking his head.

"Oh lord! I can't even ask god to help me! How can I, when the lord himself is fighting against me?!" cried Ajaya.

Once he calmed down, he joined his palms, prayed, drew his sword, and slit his own throat. Nobody reacted. Two volunteers dragged his body away to one of the tents. A single tear ran down Bheema's cheek.

"Troops! Forward march!" yelled a voice from the front. It was the commander.

"Well, see you in heaven my friend" said Pushkara in a tearful voice and the two shook hands.

"Formation: Snake!" yelled the commander.

Immediately, Bheema received a jolt from another soldier to his right.

"Move you idiot! He said snake."

Bheema moved to his left and Pushkara moved backwards. As they marched forward, he saw an arrow fly to the sky. A huge dark cloud was formed and a bolt of lightning hit the ground killing several soldiers of the enemy. This was Bheeshma's arrow.

An arrow came flying from the enemy that soon turned into a rain of fire. The soldier in front of Bheema was hit by a fire arrow and he could also hear Pushkara yell from behind him and collapse. He couldn't turn back. He stepped over the dead soldier and kept marching.

Bheeshma shot an arrow that turned into a dragon-like creature and hit the enemy. Screams of horror could be heard from the enemy.

A huge cannonball came flying from the enemy and hit the ground far behind Bheema. The sound of rocks tumbling and soldiers screaming for their lives could be heard.

Bheema closed his eyes trying to gather each and every piece of memory he had until that moment. When he was remembering his marriage, he heard the final cry from the commander.

"ATTACK!"

Bheema opened his eyes, held up his shield and sword, and ran forward, screaming at the top of his lungs. The two armies collided and the soldiers on Bheema's side were falling faster. The enemy's soldiers finally reached Bheema's line.

Bheema chopped off the head of the first soldier that tried to attack him. He stabbed another in the chest and lifted him in the air and just as he was about to throw him down, he felt a spear piercing into his back. He looked down to see a spear drenched in his own blood come out of his chest. He sighed in pain, dropped his weapons and fell to his knees.

He felt the spear being drawn out of his body and was kicked in the head. He fell face first and blacked out.

Of course, as he died, he didn't know that once the war was over, he would only be used as a stepping stone by Duryodhana, as he went to see Bheeshma and Karna. He would only be a speck of dust in the vast ocean of dead bodies in the bloody battlefield.

* * *

Gandhi Raj is Coming!

During the year 1920, in the Chikmagalur district of Karnataka, there was a large coffee plantation. As Chikmagalur was the birthplace of coffee in India, the workers in these plantations were experienced farmers. They were forced to do unimaginably hard labor as it was very important to the colonial government that they maintain its reputation in coffee exports. Under the Inland Emigration Act of 1859, the farmers were not allowed to leave their plantations and were given small huts inside the estate.

One of the workers in this plantation was Madappa. His wife Sitamma also worked here. Madappa had once been a large landowner who possessed more than fifty acres of productive land. But, due to his inability to read or write in English, he had been tricked by some British officials into signing some contracts that gave the government all his land and forced him to work in a coffee plantation. He had been devastated after realizing his hasty, stupid mistake, but had gotten over it in the fifteen years that he had worked as a plantation worker.

One evening, after a long day of hard, physical labor, Madappa was walking with his friend Thimayya to the so-called quarters.

The huts in which the workers lived were always falling apart due to the heavy rains in Chikmagalur. They had to somehow take shifts with their wives or friends to fix their huts after heavy rains.

"Well that was a rough day. Plus, I have been working 13 hour days for the last month or so and I am not getting any younger." said Madappa, wiping his sweaty face with the towel that was always on his shoulder.

"Oh, neither am I. But things are going to get a whole lot better for us folks." said Thimmayya. Thimmayya was a lean, middle aged man who knew Madappa even before they were forced into the plantations. But outside, they had been bitter rivals as both of them grew betel nuts. Inside, they had become thick friends.

"What are you talking about?" asked Madappa.

"Haven't you heard? Gandhi Raj is coming!" replied Thimmayya with his eyes shining.

"Who?"

"You don't know about Gandhi Raj? What sort of an Indian are you?" said Thimmayya teasingly as he knew he was the only one who had access to such information due to the networks he had outside the plantations.

"All right, you've had your fun. Now tell me about Gandhi Raj." said Madappa seriously.

"He is a freedom fighter."

"Oh, we have had plenty of those! They are no good."

"No no, this man is very different. He had gone to South Africa to practice law. One day, he was kicked out of a train for sitting in first class. Now, what would you have done if that had happened to you? Probably shut your mouth and walked away. But, he fought against the discrimination he and many other brown and black men were facing. And here's the interesting part: he didn't lay a finger on anyone. He fought the battle through non-violence and won!" said Thimmayya enthusiastically.

"Non – violence? How the hell did he do that? By talking to the British?" asked Madappa, fascinated.

"No, by convincing people to disobey the British and take the beatings. In the end, if the fight is against injustice, we will always win. There is a Non – Cooperation movement going on right now as we speak in the country."

"Wow! We must do something. We should be a part of this movement. Let us hold a meeting by the bonfire tonight at eleven. You inform everyone, I will address them." said Madappa.

⁎ ⁎ ⁎

Madappa entered his hut and sat by the door.

"Ree (it was a custom for wives to call their husbands by this word in Karnataka), what took you so long?" asked Sitamma – Madappa's wife – handing him a glass of water.

Sitamma and Madappa had been married for twenty years, that is five years before being exiled in the plantation. They could never have children. But somehow, in the plantation, it didn't seem to matter to them as much as it did outside. Sitamma always spoke to her husband angrily as if she despised him and never wanted to spend her life with him, but she had always loved him.

"Listen, we have arranged a meeting tonight at eleven. It is really important. This might be our way out." said Madappa, excited.

"What? Slow down! Tell me what is going on." said Sitamma and sat down.

Madappa told her everything Thimmayya had told him and she was overjoyed. She could not believe that after fifteen years, they could walk out these wretched gates to freedom.

That night, Madappa, Sitamma and Thimmayya had assembled by the bonfire before everyone else. They had only about two hours to hold these meetings. The night shift guards would arrive at one in the morning.

"Are you sure you called everyone?" asked Madappa, impatiently.

"Yes, and that is the third time you've asked me that." replied Thimmayya, calmly.

"Then why isn't anyone here yet?!" said Madappa, thumping his foot on the ground.

"Ree, you're being stupid! Have some patience." said Sitamma.

"Here they are!" said Thimmayya.

Slowly – one by one – the workers started gathering around the fire. In a few minutes, everybody was there. There were about a hundred of them.

Thimmayya looked at Madappa and nodded. Madappa went and stood by the fire and cleared his throat. All the murmurs stopped.

"So, how many of you have heard of Gandhi Raj?" said Madappa.

There was no answer.

"How many of you know that there is a Non – Cooperation movement going on outside these gates? The whole country is defying the British and he is the great man who is leading the country."

Suddenly, there was an outbreak of chattering and murmuring in the crowd.

"Silence!" yelled Thimmayya.

"So, what do you propose we do, Madappa? If you're saying we need to defy these guards, I think it's too risky." yelled a voice from the crowd.

"I propose we do what our country requires us to do. I propose we fight back. We have been slaves to these white foreigners for too long. If we don't fight for our motherland, who will? For the first time, we have an opportunity to live in freedom. It is time, my friends. We must now stop being submissive and start intimidating!" said Madappa. The reflection of the fire danced in his eyes.

There was a brief silence. Then, the crowd was suddenly transformed. All of them raised their fists and fire torches.

"Gandhi Raj, Zindabad!!!" shouted the crowd.

This was not what Madappa and Thimmayya had in mind, but the sight of this new energy they had just created did something to them. It gave them a new sense of power.

"ATTACK!!!" yelled Madappa and motioned everyone to run towards the gate. Suddenly, the quiet atmosphere of the plantations had transformed to an extremely violent one. The workers set fire to the plantation as they went along.

By the time they reached the gate, a few guards had been informed to take care of this as the fire had been sighted. Ten guards stood in a perfectly horizontal line before the gate.

"Don't move or we will open fire!" said one of the guards. But, the workers could not be stopped. They kept running forward.

"FIRE!!!"

Shots were fired and more than twenty of the workers were killed. But, even the bullets were not enough. The workers furiously ran forward and burnt the guards alive!

They ran out the gates behind Madappa who had now turned into a beast, drunk with the fantasy of freedom. He hadn't even noticed that both Sitamma and Thimmayya had been killed.

They kept marching, shouting: "Gandhi Raj, Zindabad!!!"

Soon, it was dawn and the sun was rising. They had marched for hours with the same energy, setting fire to anything in sight. They saw the railway station in the distance and Madappa directed the workers towards it.

As soon as they entered the railway station, they were in a world of confusion. The workers in the station were conducting a strike. There were thousands of people protesting and British troops had just been called in.

"Everybody, stand down! Move aside!" yelled a British official.

The plantation workers, however, were very confused and didn't know what to do. They kept shouting.

"Gandhi Raj! Gandhi Raj! Gandhi Raj!"

The sight of fire enraged the troops and they didn't think twice.

"FIRE!!!"

The guns started firing away.

Madappa looked around, searching for his wife and best friend. It was too late. A bullet struck him in the chest and he fell to the ground. The last few things he saw were his fellow workers get shot and be beaten up brutally.

Well, Gandhi Raj hadn't come after all.

Over-Arm

In 1812, there lived a boy named Joseph Weller in south-east England. He was an orphan and had no home. He sold newspapers in the morning and roamed the streets for the rest of the day. He would sleep on the bench outside a church nearby. He had only one friend who was the son of a wood-cutter. Both of them would walk on the wet roads and buy street food with Joseph's money. Their favorite thing to do on a sunny day was watching a few people in the park play this local new game called Cricket. This game fascinated Joseph immensely. There were two teams and each had roughly ten members.

This game was to be played on a large field. In the center of this field were three sticks standing vertically, parallel to each other. Exactly opposite to these, a few meters away were three more such sticks. One team would have its members scattered on the field and they would take turns standing next to one group of the sticks and rolling a small round ball towards the other group of sticks. In front of this group of sticks, a member from the opponent team would be standing holding a thicker stick in his hands to hit the ball. Once the ball was hit, two players from the hitting team would run between the two groups of sticks, and all the others from the throwing team would be running around in all directions in pursuit of the ball. All the other members of the hitting team would be sitting and watching. If the ball hit any of the standing sticks, one of the hitters would come back and another would go to the ground to replace him. The hitting team was called the 'batting' team and the throwing team was called the 'bowling' team. After some time, the teams would exchange their jobs.

This was how Joseph had first perceived the game. However, after a few months, he understood it in great detail and explained it to his friend George five times so as to give him some level of understanding.

One day, both of them decided to join these people to play. They went to the field and Joseph boldly went to the players to ask if they could join.

"Excuse me, sir" he said to one of the members of the batting team.

All of the players looked at him awkwardly. George began to have second thoughts.

"Can I help you?" asked one of the players in a rude tone.

"Uh…I was wondering if…we could join you to play", Joseph stammered.

"We?" asked the player.

"Yes, me and my…" Joseph looked back to see that George was nowhere in sight. All the players started laughing at Joseph. He was red with embarrassment.

"Get out of here, kid" shouted another player.

Joseph walked away, disappointed. He spotted George on the way.

"Why would you ditch me like that, George?" said Joseph angrily.

"Did you see those men? They could have beaten us to a pulp! We can't play with them" replied George.

"We will play! Let us make our own equipment" said Joseph.

George hesitated.

"Your father is a wood-cutter, isn't he? He must be able to help", said Joseph.

"All right!", said George, finally convinced.

The next afternoon, the boys were sitting under a tree making their very own cricket equipment. They had got George's father to make the stumps and the ball, but he wouldn't help them with the bat. Joseph tried a lot to make the bat look like the original, but failed miserably! They ended up taking a flat plank of wood and calling it a bat. Another group of boys saw them making the bat and wanted to join them to play. Joseph and George accepted happily. Soon all of the boys headed into the woods, found a clearing and hammered the stumps into the ground. They soon divided each other into two teams. Joseph was the first batsman and George was the first bowler. George rolled the ball and Joseph hit it. The ball rolled straight to George's hands. The same thing happened the next two balls. Joseph was getting annoyed. He wanted to make the game more exciting. Suddenly, he had an idea.

"Hey George, this time, throw the ball directly instead of rolling it," he said.

"What?!"

"You heard me!"

"Fine, mate," replied George.

George threw the ball and it came through the air towards Joseph. Joseph came forward and swung the bat, hitting the ball with all his might. The ball went flying out of sight! All the boys started shouting and cheering for Joseph with excitement. They had never seen something this extraordinary. Joseph did the same thing the next few balls before he got out as his palms started slipping. He then customized the bat by making the part where he held the bat narrower. He called this the handle. He improved day by day at hitting these shots. Until then, the maximum runs you could score in one ball was four. The town players called Joseph's shot "The six runner". Joseph was soon famous throughout the town. People called him "The young innovator". Fifty years later, the game Joseph had innovated was being played internationally. Two-hundred years later, it was one of the world's most celebrated sports.

* * *

The Mirror Man

Agrahara was a village located at the heart of the Western Ghats in Karnataka. This village was isolated from other villages. The two main occupations of people in this village were hunting and betel nut farming.

The farmers of Agrahara were richer than the hunters. This was because betel nuts were of great demand and were expensive. Not many people ate meat in Agrahara.

In the stories of these villagers, there was an interesting character called the Mirror Man. He wore a black cloak with a hood and his face was covered by a mirror.

But, what was more fascinating about the Mirror Man was, in the stories of the hunters, he was a savior who helped people when they were in need. In the stories of the farmers, he was a villainous demon who haunted people and robbed them of their wealth.

The elders of the village always used to say that he had lived in this village for over 250 years. Many people had claimed to have seen him when they were walking alone on their fields or in the forest. But most people in Agrahara, especially the farmers, did not believe in his existence.

Chanakya was a boy who lived in Agrahara and was the son of the biggest farmer in the village. Ever since he was a child, he was told the stories of the Mirror Man by his mother. Although he was told numerous times that they were all just stories and the Mirror Man didn't actually exist, he was a strong believer. Every night, he dreamt of the Mirror Man punishing the bad farmers of his village who troubled the poor hunters. By the time he was fifteen years-old, he became obsessed with the Mirror Man. To prove his existence, he would sit outside his house in the dark all night waiting for the Mirror Man to show up. He did this many times until he realized that it wouldn't work. So, he thought of a better plan.

One foggy night, he stepped out of his window and started walking towards his father's field. He had gone there many times with his father to understand the process of farming. He loved going there – not to understand farming, but to see the scarecrows. He kept walking, shining his torch in every direction. When he finally reached the field, he sat down on a bench. His plan was to go a good distance in and wait for the Mirror Man to show up. After a few minutes of rest, he got up and started walking again. His father's field was about six acres big and was right next to the forest. Chanakya remembered that his father always complained about wild boars from the forest destroying his crops. Chanakya was walking about fifty meters away from the beginning of the forest. Suddenly, he heard the noise of a bush shaking, clearly, in the silence of the night. He turned towards the forest. He could see a bush shaking and the next second, something came out of it and started walking towards the inside of the forest. Chanakya immediately started running in, making the least noise possible, with butterflies in his stomach.

By the time he reached the forest, he could clearly make out the figure of a man wearing a cloak and a hood walking towards an abandoned hut. Chanakya slowly followed the man making no noise, hiding behind every tree and bush in the way. But now, for some strange reason, Chanakya's attitude towards the Mirror Man changed. He remembered how he robbed and tortured the farmers by burning their houses and fields at night. He started to regret coming here and wanted to go back home. But, somehow, his legs didn't allow him to turn back, it kept moving forward.

By now, they were close to the hut. Suddenly, an ear shattering scream of a man came from the hut and made Chanakya freeze. A few seconds later, a man ran out of the hut. His white shirt was covered in blood, and blood was dripping from the sickle in his hand! So alarmed was Chanakya that he couldn't even scream.

When the man with the sickle saw the cloaked man, his expression turned from anger to that of fear. He threw the sickle at the cloaked man and started running. The cloaked man dodged, drew a sharp knife from his belt and threw it at the running man. The knife pierced through the back of his neck and he collapsed without any noise.

The cloaked man, turning around and revealing his mirrored face, saw Chanakya.

"Who are you?" asked Chanakya, shivering.

"I am the Mirror Man, you must have heard of me." replied the Mirror Man with his muffled voice behind the mirror.

"Why did you kill that man?" asked Chanakya.

"That man was a bad person. He killed a laborer just because he demanded extra pay." replied the Mirror Man.

"Why didn't you kill me?" asked Chanakya.

"You? You are not a bad person, are you? You are just a curious little child. There is no reason for me to kill you." said the Mirror Man.

"You should be proud of what you are doing. Why do you cover your face? Why a mirror?" asked Chanakya, confused.

"Proud? Of what? I told you that that man was a bad person, a murderer, which is why I killed him. But what about me? Didn't I kill him? Am I not a bad person too? That is why I cover my face with a mirror. When people see me, I want them to see themselves. When people try to judge me, I want them to judge themselves."

"But why do people say that you don't exist?" asked Chanakya, still not satisfied.

"If you want me to exist, I exist, if not, I don't exist. Now why would some people say that I don't exist? Maybe because they are guilty of their crimes. Now, enough questions." said the Mirror Man and vanished.

Chanakya was lying down on his bed, looking out of the window, imagining himself twenty years from now, telling this story to his children. Would he tell them about the Mirror Man? Would he tell them that the Mirror Man existed?

* * *

Dog Nation

There is a flat piece of land in the outskirts of Bangalore. It used to be a forest once, but now most of it has been cleared. It has now been converted partially into a landfill. It is also a city in itself – of stray dogs. There are multiple packs of stray dogs here that howl endlessly at night and have their battles between packs. People living close to this area prefer not to come out at night. But, that night was an exception.

Three men – two of which looked slightly like thugs and the third looked decent enough – were walking on the so-called 'road' in the middle of this area. The road was full of potholes and humps due to lack of maintenance. But, none of that seemed to matter to them right now. One of these three people was a new politician who was contesting the upcoming MLA elections. He had come here to meet a few members of another party in order to make a deal and sign a few contracts. The other two men had come to watch his back and ensure that nothing went wrong. These two looked similar to each other. Their names were Manja and Ranga. Manja was slightly smaller than Ranga. Both of them had tucked in long sickles at the back of their shirts. The name of their boss was Chowriappa. They kept walking and the dogs that were going through the garbage had their eyes on them.

After sometime, when a broken bench came into sight, they stopped and Chowriappa sat down.

"This is the place," said Chowriappa.

"They aren't here yet," said Manja.

"Have some patience, you fool," said Ranga, looking at Manja.

They waited for about half an hour and suddenly, a big, white Fortuner car pulled up in front of them.

"They're here." said Manja.

The driver of the Fortuner got out and opened the door of the front passenger seat. The man who got out had at least five gold chains around his neck and gold rings on all his fingers. Next, three bodyguards got out of the back seat. These bodyguards had similar outfits as Manja and Ranga, except for the pistols tucked into their trousers. Their weapons and strength in numbers made Chowriappa and his men feel a little insecure.

"You are late, Somaiyya. We have been waiting for almost thirty minutes." said Chowriappa, walking towards the men.

"Oh, really?" asked Somaiyya, sarcastically.

"What's with so many bodyguards? I thought we agreed on bringing two each" said Chowriappa.

"Oh yes, I wasn't sure if two were enough," replied Somaiyya, smiling.

"I hope you have the contracts ready," said Chowriappa.

"Of course" replied Somaiyya and his driver handed him some papers. Manja and Ranga looked at each other as they could not make out much of what was going on. Somaiyya gave these papers to Chowriappa and as he went through them, one by one, his expression changed.

"What the hell is all this? We didn't agree to all this!" shouted Chowriappa.

"Shut up and sign them!" said Somaiyya and one of his bodyguards took out his pistol and aimed it at Chowriappa's head.

Ranga reckoned that this was his time to shine. He drew out his sickle and hit the bodyguard with all his might! The bodyguard fell to the ground, dropping his gun, crying in pain. Another bodyguard immediately took out his pistol and shot Ranga in the head! Chowriappa and Manja started running for their lives. The bodyguards started firing. Two bullets hit Manja in his leg, making him collapse. But, Chowriappa escaped from the bullets and hid behind a wrecked car.

He could hear the dogs – that were silent till then – barking, and Manja screaming in pain.

"What are you dimwits standing here for!? Go and find him!" Somaiyya yelled at his bodyguards.

"I will give you five seconds to come out before I kill your man! One, two, three, four, five!"

Chowriappa heard a gunshot and Manja's screams stopped abruptly. Suddenly, he heard a soft growl next to him. He looked and saw a big, black dog growling.

"No! Please……shh" he whispered.

The dog started barking its head off and jumped towards Chowriappa! He ran out of his hiding place, now in clear sight of Somaiyya. Somaiyya didn't seem to think twice. He immediately snatched a gun from one of his bodyguards and shot Chowriappa twice in the chest.

Chowriappa sighed and fell to the ground. The last thing he heard was the Fortuner driving away. He stared at the sky as the full moon came out from behind the clouds and shed light on the four dead bodies.

Then, finally, the howling of the dogs began.

* * *

Hunger

Vikram was a prosperous man living in the metropolitan city of Bangalore. He had always been a successful person. Even as a child, he scored good grades at school and played the piano very well. When his teachers asked him what he wanted to do when he grew up, he said he wanted to make a lot of money. When asked what he would do with his money, he'd say that he would use it to make more money. He was seen as a bright person by everyone around him.

He grew up to be an engineer and got employed in one of the most reputed software companies. He soon got married, had two children – a girl and a boy – and bought a big mansion. His wife, Lakshmi ensured that his money was spent well. They had two high end Mercedes cars. Life was going well for Vikram. He never stopped playing the piano. It was his favorite hobby. When he was stressed, it would always relax him.

But, every night, as he tried to sleep, he felt he hadn't reached his goal. He hadn't made enough money.

This led him to get into the real estate business. It gave him the atmosphere he had always thrived in.

"That builder has five BMWs, I want six."

One day, Vikram came back from dinner at a restaurant in UB city and went to his room to practice his piano. His family wasn't at home as Lakshmi had taken the children to their grandparents. He kept on playing, unaware of his surroundings. He didn't hear the main door and his office door open and a bike ride away. After he finished playing, he went to his office to get his laptop so that he could do a video chat with his family, but to his horror, he couldn't find it! He searched the entire house and later realized that the main door was unlocked. He immediately called the police and informed them about his missing laptop.

"Please don't worry sir, we'll see what we can do." replied the police.

The next day he was at the house of one of his colleagues, sitting in his living room, sipping coffee. This colleague's name was Kiran. He too was in the real estate business. But that wasn't the reason Vikram was here. Kiran was a famous underground arms dealer.

"So, Vikram, it has been a long time since we have met, or even talked. How is the family? Most importantly, to what do I owe the pleasure of meeting you?" asked Kiran.

"You know why I'm here." replied Vikram.

"Of course I do, but what's the hurry? You have come to meet me after such a long time, let's have a chat." said Kiran.

"You don't have to pretend you like me." replied Vikram.

"Oh, you only got me fired once. That is a perfectly acceptable thing to do. Why should I despise you or anything like that?" asked Kiran sarcastically.

"Look, let's leave all that in the past. I'm sorry for what I did. Now let's get to the real deal. How much would that Beretta M9 cost me?" asked Vikram, pointing at a showcase of pistols that Kiran had near his staircase.

"Five hundred grand. Not a buck less." replied Kiran, quickly.

"Okay, I am not even going to negotiate with you. When can you have it delivered?" asked Vikram, smiling with excitement.

"It will take about a week." said Kiran.

"Fine."

"But why can't you get a license? You were all about not taking risks, weren't you?" asked Kiran.

"Not anymore." replied Vikram, keeping his coffee cup on the table.

"I will pay a hundred grand in advance and the rest once it is delivered."

"Hundred? I need at least fifty percent. This isn't a normal delivery." said Kiran.

"All right." replied Vikram

Both of them shook hands and Vikram left.

The next day, Vikram was in the Police station.

"So, officer, tell me about my laptop. Were you able to find those brats?" asked Vikram.

"We still haven't been able to track your computer, sir. We will let you know once we have some updates." replied the inspector.

"What? How much time is this going to take? Do you know the value of what's on my laptop? You wouldn't understand. Don't you have *any* updates?" asked Vikram, furiously.

"It isn't child's play to find a small thing like a laptop in this city, sir."

Vikram got livid and left the station.

The Beretta M9 arrived exactly a week later and Vikram kept it securely in a locker. His wife didn't at all approve of having the gun. She was very angry at the fact that Vikram had made such a decision without asking her. Vikram somehow managed to calm her down.

The next few months weren't the best for Vikram. He had quit his software job and had gotten full time into the real estate business. However, it wasn't a good decision as he was suffering losses and was heavily in debt. He had already sold both of his Mercedes cars and had downgraded to a Honda City. What was worse was that he hadn't told his family about him quitting his job, so he was still spending a lot of money on other things.

One day, he got back home, frustrated and went to his room to practice his piano. He started playing and went on for about ten minutes. His head was filled with worries. He couldn't focus, his fingers kept touching the wrong keys. He got agitated and toppled the piano.

His wife and children came rushing into his room.

"What the hell happened?" asked Lakshmi.

"Nothing, it was just a minor accident, I'm fine though." Vikram replied not making eye contact.

"Are you sure?" asked Lakshmi.

"I said I'm fine!" shouted Vikram.

Lakshmi was frightened. Her husband had never shouted at her like that. Even the kids were confused.

"Come, children. Dad is not in a good mood now." said Lakshmi to the kids and took them out of the room.

Right after they left the room, Vikram's phone started ringing. He looked at the phone to see who was calling him. It was another one of his colleagues who he had borrowed money from. Vikram didn't answer. As soon as the phone stopped ringing, he received a voice message from the colleague.

"Hey, it's been six months now. If I don't hear back from you by tomorrow, there's gonna be consequences."

The next day, after dinner, Vikram's family was sitting in the hall, watching T.V. He walked in and switched it off.

"Hey, what did you do that for?" asked his son.

"Be quiet, Surya, I have something important to say to you guys." said Vikram and sat down.

"What is it, Vikram?" asked Lakshmi.

"So, what I'm about to say will shock you, but please don't get mad at me." said Vikram and told them about him quitting his job a few months ago and that he was in heavy debt.

"That's why you sold the cars. Now what do you suppose we do about this?" asked Lakshmi.

Vikram took a deep breath.

"You are not going to like this, but I have come to a decision that we have to sell this house." said Vikram, and by seeing the look on Lakshmi's face he knew he was doomed.

"What? Are you crazy? Where the hell are we going to live then?" shouted Lakshmi standing up.

"I still need to figure that out." replied Vikram.

"Are you out of your bloody mind? You want to sell this house and you don't even know where we are going to live? Why do you take these big decisions without even consulting your own damn family? First, you go and buy a gun, then you quit your job, and now you want to sell your damn house! What the hell is going on with you?"

"Dad bought a gun?" asked Surya and Rashmi – the kids – simultaneously.

"Shut up! This isn't the time. Go to your rooms!" ordered Lakshmi.

The kids looked at each other, got up and went.

"I am telling you right now, Vikram, do what you want but you are NOT selling this house!" said Lakshmi.

Vikram sighed and said: "Okay." He got up and went to his room.

"What? What do you mean 'okay'? What are you going to do?" asked Lakshmi as Vikram walked away. She didn't get any response. Vikram had a plan.

Everybody went to sleep as usual.

At exactly twelve at midnight, Vikram got up from his bed. He went to his office room, and opened his safe. Then, he took out his Beretta M9 and smiled demonically. He loaded it with four bullets and went to his bedroom.

Lakshmi woke up, hearing Vikram cocking the gun, and switched on the lights.

"What's wrong? Is somebody here?" she asked. She saw an unearthly look on Vikram's face that she had never seen before.

"Vikram, Is everything okay?" she asked in a trembling voice.

"No. NOTHING IS OKAY!" said Vikram in a devil-like voice. He raised his gun and shot his wife in the head. The children heard the noise and came running upstairs to see their mother lying dead, blood all over the room and their father holding a gun, staring at them.

The children didn't think twice. They ran downstairs and out of the house screaming for help.

Vikram chased after them.

"Don't worry, children! Daddy is here to save you!" he screamed as he ran outside on the street. He fired two bullets. One missed and one rubbed against Surya's shoulder. He shrieked in pain!

Two police jeeps rolled up at the end of the street and the children were taken in by an officer. Two policemen got out.

"Mr. Vikram, you are under arrest, put down your weapon immediately!" shouted one of them and both were pointing their pistols at him.

Vikram fell to his knees. He had just one more bullet in his gun. He looked up, shot himself in the throat and blood splashed out from the back of his head. He was lying dead on the road. An ambulance was called to take him, and the children were first taken to the hospital. After Surya's shoulder was treated, they were taken to their grandparents' house.

* * *

The Director's Nightmare

Chandra Kumar was a director in Bangalore. He was one of the most famous directors in the Sandalwood film industry. He enjoyed his job a lot. He was also very proud of his works as only he would write the scripts for his films. He took writing very seriously and made it abundantly clear by getting a house built in the middle of a forest. He lived mainly in the city, but went to the forest house only when he had to write. There was only one thing about his job that he hated, and this was hiring actors. He never hired reputed actors. He preferred having auditions and selecting new ones. He was extremely particular about the acting, so it took him weeks to finalize his selections.

Today was one of those days. He sat in his office with his hair all messed up, conducting the auditions. Today, he was looking for the antagonist of his film, an old man who is a psychopath and in the end, kills his entire family and himself.

It was six in the evening and Chandra hadn't been happy with anyone. He was tired, so he told everyone that he would continue tomorrow and left. He got into his car, took his phone out, called his wife and told her that he will be staying at the forest house. He was about to close his car door when he realized that the boot was unlocked. He immediately closed it and started driving towards his cottage.

Once he reached, he called his assistant who lived near the forest house.

"Hello?"

"Yes sir?"

"Raghunath, I am starving. Get the dinner delivered as soon as possible. I'll leave the door unlocked."

"Sure, sir."

Chandra went to the fridge, took a beer bottle and went upstairs, to his office room. A while later, he heard the door open.

"You took quite a long time, Raghunath" shouted Chandra.

But, he didn't get any response. Assuming that Raghunath wanted to leave as soon as possible as it was late, Chandra went downstairs. When he reached the dining room, he saw Raghunath arranging the dinner and asked him why he didn't respond.

"Oh, I couldn't hear you, sir" replied Raghunath and hurried back home.

Chandra switched on the T.V and started eating his dinner. Suddenly, he heard footsteps from the bathroom.

"Raghunath, haven't you left yet?" he shouted. No response.

"Raghunath, is that you?" Still nothing.

Chandra got up and went to the bathroom. Just when he was about to reach for the door handle, the lights went out.

"Oh shit!" shouted Chandra, agitated.

He took out his phone and turned on the flashlight. He could hear frogs and crickets of the forest making noise, an owl hooting and a dog howling in the distance. Suddenly, someone ran across the dining room behind Chandra. He immediately turned around, startled. He could hear someone climbing the stairs. He went towards the staircase and stepped on the first stair. The creaking sound that it made was unusually loud. Suddenly, he got a text message. Of course, he ignored it. He took another step, and to his astonishment, he got another text. Another step and a third text. Finally, he turned his phone on and read three texts saying,

"DO NOT FOLLOW ME !!!"

This scared the living hell out of him.

"WHO ARE YOU?" he shouted.

"Get out of here or I'll call the police!"

After hearing nothing, he dialed one,zero,zero on his phone and waited for the police to answer. Suddenly, the piano in his office started playing! He could hear disturbing notes. Chandra had had enough. He immediately went to the top of the staircase and suddenly, something came flying towards him and hit him in the face! He fell backwards, rolled down the stairs and fell on his front, crying in pain. He quickly got up, ran towards the main door and frantically tried to open it. But, it just wouldn't open. He could hear an old man's voice from upstairs, approaching him, crying and repeatedly saying:

"LOOK WHAT YOU MADE ME DO!"

Chandra ran to the back door and tried to open it, but in vain. He could hear footsteps approaching him and the crying getting louder.

He turned around and saw one of the most terrifying things he had ever seen in his life! An old man, covered in blood, holding a dagger and screaming:

"LOOK WHAT YOU MADE ME DO!!!"

Chandra ran upstairs as fast as he could, went to his office room and grabbed his cricket bat. Then he started running downstairs, when his phone died and his flashlight – that was working all this while – went out. He tripped over something, and while he was falling, his bat slipped from his hand and fell a few feet away.

The old man appeared from nowhere, holding the dagger! Chandra tried getting up, but his leg seemed to be broken.

"Help! Somebody, help me!" shouted Chandra at the top of his lungs. But, Raghunath was his closest neighbor who lived at least a couple miles away and was fast asleep.

The old man, to Chandra's astonishment, put the dagger down and said something that Chandra would never forget in his life.

"So, Mr. Kumar, did I do well?"

* * *

About the Author

Bhaasita Athani is 19 years old and he is currently studying film production at Srishti Manipal Institute of Art, Design and Technology, Bangalore. Apart from writing short stories and novellas, his interests include making short films and urban photography. He lives in Bangalore, India.

www.ingramcontent.com/pod-product-compliance
Lightning Source LLC
Chambersburg PA
CBHW062219150726
47991CB00006B/2348